I0530094

THE WAR HORSE

BARB SIMMONS

Copyright © 2025 by Barb Simmons

This is a work of fiction. Names, characters, organizations, places, events, and incidents are either products of the author's imagination or are used fictitiously. No part of this work was generated by artificial intelligence technologies.

All rights reserved.

No part of this book may be reproduced, or stored in a retrieval system, or transmitted in any form or by any electronic or mechanical means, including information storage and retrieval systems, without written permission from the author, except for the use of brief quotations in a book review.

No part of this book may be used in any manner for purposes of training artificial intelligence technologies to generate text or audio, including without limitation, technologies that are capable of generating works in the same style or genre as this work without the specific and express permission from the author.

Cover by Spittyfish Designs

Acknowledgments

Every book/story is a journey, and the writer is never alone on that journey. Many people along the way have helped out in many different ways, and more than they realize. This is my opportunity to thank you, one and all.

I was lucky to become acquainted with Rick, a Vietnam era Marine, through a high school friend. He was a great help in setting and intensity.

My only research visit/trip for this book, was to Enchanted Equine Adventures, owned and operated by Kendra Loring. Spent a lovely afternoon at her facility reacquainting myself with the horse world.

Thank you, Tanya, for reading for me *again*. You're the best.

I so appreciate you for your editing prowess and on-going encouragement, Carol. Lions all the way!!!

Big time gratitude to Janice Mary for the proofing, and monitoring my horse language and references. Ride on, Sister!!!

A special thank-you to my oldest friend, Kristy, who lent me her name for my heroine. Will never forget our ongoing sessions of hopscotch out front, on Clinton Street.

Thank you, Sheley, my extraordinary critique partner and friend of many years, who listened patiently and gave me clarity, as I skipped and swayed through my worries and woes writing this story.

And lastly, my husband Charlie, who is there for me always, and then some. You're the best decision I ever made.

*My deepest apologies to anyone who helped me, who is not present on the list.

To
Katie and Patty
My beloved and wonderful sisters.

THE WAR HORSE

Chapter 1

Parking his grocery cart in the middle of the aisle, Trevor Drury whipped his chair around and sped back to the end of the row to get some bread. He grabbed a loaf of 7-grain and spun around, launching a free-throw shot at his basket.

Oh, no, no, no! Oh, shit!

He stared in horror as the bread arched beautifully, then overshot the basket, hitting the woman standing beside his cart right in the side of her head. It bounced off her thick gold-and-silver hair, landing in his cart with a resounding plop.

She turned and glared at him with a hard stare that would singe skin to smoking. Immediately her gaze morphed into something else, into something somewhat open and amiable. Something maybe a little curious, even.

Unless he was at the gym, that didn't happen to him very often because: one, he was no spring rooster and two, he used a wheelchair to get around. Losing his legs in Vietnam had left him a permanent member of the wheelie crew.

"I'm so sorry about that," he said whizzing back toward her and the cart. "I thought I was alone in the aisle—at least I was when I headed over to the bread." He leaned back in his

1

chair, focusing on her huge sky-blue eyes. *Absolutely stunning.* "You're quick."

"I *have* been told that I sneak up on people," she said with a sly smile. "No harm, I needed something to jolt me into focus anyway." She laughed and returned her attention to the cookies she'd been eyeing with noticeable longing the moment she was beaned.

She reached up and teased out a package of the Grande Chocolate Chip brand, then looking back at him, she said, "My kryptonite."

He wheeled gently closer, stopping with his shopping cart between them. "Mine's dark chocolate." Jesus, he had to think of more to say, to keep her right where she stood. "But I've been known to do some damage to a package of those."

She looked down at him, her brows pulled down in skepticism, her huge blue eyes shining bright. "You don't look like you dally much with frivolous carbs."

Ah nice, a compliment, he grinned. "I just finished prep and a body-building competition this past weekend. I'm a little leaner than usual."

The moment those words left his mouth, a storm warning covered her features and the temperature around them dropped a good twenty degrees.

"Have a nice day," she said with no real feeling and turned away. She marched off, turning left at the end of the aisle, disappearing out of sight.

"What the hell?" he murmured to himself, straightening in his chair. What just happened?

———

ANOTHER SELF-ABSORBED JERK. KRISTY SHOULD have flashed to that the moment she saw him. All that bicep poking out from below his sleeves, pecs pressing against his navy-blue T-shirt, minute lingering traces of competition spray tan.

Ugh! Never again. She'd let the fact that he had bilateral above-the-knee amputations soften her thinking, but only for a moment. Yeah, just because he had a disability didn't guarantee the guy wasn't a tool.

Clearing her thoughts, she focused on her remaining errands. When she got back to Bosque Farms, she needed to go to the feed store for a few more sacks of rolled oats and then stop by the vet to pick up more meds for Agnes, one of her bullmastiffs. Aggie's allergies were picking up like crazy with the fall weather. Who would have thought her one-hundred-twenty-pound lap dog would have turned out to be such a delicate flower?

She pulled into the feed store parking lot and backed right up to the open semi on autopilot. When she got inside, there was no line at the counter, so she was in and out of there quickly. The guy in the semi tossed the three oat sacks into the bed of her black F150 and off she went to the vet.

Her little Ranchito was a mile off the loop in Bosque Farms, just south of Albuquerque, and she loved that. So peaceful, so still. No constant passage of vehicles. The way her three acres were situated, a car would only be coming near her house, if they were intentionally visiting. She loved her place, her private hideaway.

Whenever she headed home, the instant she pulled off Highway 47 onto Bosque Loop, she could feel her stress level drop. Then, when she turned from the Loop onto her road, relaxation took over. Any remaining angst dropped off nicely, until it dissipated completely as she turned on to her tree-lined drive.

Her small occupational therapy practice, where she focused on equine therapy, was her pride and joy. Her work provided her a decent living while doing what she really loved, really believed in—helping people with disabilities get stronger, feel more confident, and better able to negotiate their world. Of course, with the assistance of her wonderful horses-- Sugar, Stormy, and Houdini.

She pulled up to her gate and got out to open it. Aggie bounded up to greet her. She scratched her dog behind the ears telling her what a great girl she was, before opening the door of the truck for Aggie to hop in and ride back to the house with her as was often their routine.

As they pulled up to the house Baxter, her older, less demonstrative mastiff, raised his giant head from his guarding position of lounging by the front door, and gave them his customary three bark greeting but didn't bother to get up.

"Hey Baxter," she offered. The response he gave sounded like he was clearing his throat, before dropping his head back down to his massive, crossed paws.

Kristy laughed, then took her purchases into the house. She set her two string grocery bags on the kitchen table and looked over at the answering machine. The number three blinked on and off.

Her friends laughed at her, still using a landline and an answering machine. But she liked that just fine. She could decide whether she answered the phone, and who and when she spoke to anyone. An essential part of her quest for privacy. The set-up was just right for her reality, thank you very much. She did own a cell phone, but it sat on her desk a lot of the time.

After going back out to dump the oats into the bin in her tack room, she checked on and fed the horses. The nick on Houdini's right hock was almost healed up. At twenty-six, he was the oldest and most cantankerous of her horses. Other than herself and her assistant, he did not care for most adults, especially men. But the kids—the sight of a child turned him into a giant mush-ball, dropping his head and gently rubbing his cheek against them whenever he could. A gray thorough-bred, he was one of those horses she could always count on in the ring with the kids. Performed like a champ during their sessions.

But he hated being confined. Didn't mind contending with the elements one bit as long as he was in a space at least the size of her smaller circular riding ring, the one she had most of her sessions in. He'd gotten the nick when she'd taken him to the vet last week for his yearly shots. He and the horse trailer were not at all compatible. All his dancing around in there had resulted in that cut.

She'd engage Dr. Jernigan for next year's vaccinations. She made house calls.

The guy from Nature Mart jumped in and landed center stage in her mind's eye. A spectacular, stark image of him sitting in his chair—naked to the waist. All that defined and amazing muscle, hot and damp from exercise. His biceps and shoulders flexed as he adjusted himself in his chair.

Oh, my God. Kristy swallowed. Hard. Where did that come from? He was *not* a guy she should be thinking about. Not at all. *No way!*

Houdini nickered, pulling her thinking to where it should be. Between the bars of the pipe fencing, she scratched under his forelock while he ate.

When she entered her house again, she headed for the blinking answering machine and pressed the button to get her messages. The first want to sell her stucco, and the second lend her money. The third was Steve Murphy, the community support guy for Rob Chavez, one of her clients. "Hey Kristy, I'm going on vacation for a couple of weeks. Just wanted to let you know, someone else will be bringing Rob to his sessions while I'm gone. His name is Trevor."

Aww, what a nice guy, to step up like that, Kristy thought absently as she opened the fridge to forage for dinner.

CHAPTER 2

L ater that week Trevor wheeled through the glass doors into the gym, nodding to the two youngsters behind the front desk, which had already been decorated for Halloween by late September. *Jesus! Why are people in such a damn hurry?*

He headed to the back of the huge expanse, to the free-weight area. His body and mind acclimating to what he was about to do for the next two hours. The welcome cacophony of bang and clang a vital part of getting his head in the right place.

Spying the guys, he was glad to see them already assembled and at it, in their usual spot.

Steve, Rob, and Mike. Rob had Down syndrome, Mike, a former Marine Raider, lost a leg in Afghanistan, and Steve's work was to help make life a little easier for people with disabilities. Common goals, brothers, although at his age he felt like the older uncle. Maybe even the granddad. *Nope! Nope.* He wasn't ready to go there, yet. He chuckled to himself.

Although he *was* considered the official father's side

grandpa to Mike and Vivian's little girl, Sophie. That was different. Mike's folks passed when he was a kid.

As he approached their band of brothers, Mike gave him the high sign.

"So, what's everyone working on today?"

Rob jumped up from the bench he'd been sitting on. He tilted his head to the side and jammed his hands on his hips. "Trevor, it's Wednesday, we always do upper body on Wednesday."

Trevor grinned. "Ok, ok. You're right on the money, Rob."

"That's Mr. Rob to you," the younger man said, with a haughty but playful expression on his face.

"Yes, sir," Trevor said saluting. That guy had developed all kinds of confidence since he'd joined him and Mike at the gym. It was so great to see.

Trevor grabbed a five-foot length of PVC pipe that leaned against the wall next to a rack of dumbbells and rolled over to an empty bench. Then he transferred onto the bench, straddled it with his stumps, and proceeded to use the pipe to methodically stretch his shoulders, arms and back. He'd learned long ago what happened when he didn't warm up properly. *Pain.* The arthritis in his neck and shoulders was bad enough, he didn't need to tack on anything else.

Dropping the pipe to the side of his bench when he'd finished stretching, he called out to Steve. "Hey, could you hand me one of those thirty-five pounders?"

"Sure." The guy went over to the rack and with his right hand he hoisted up the dumbbell and brought it over, setting it easily in front of Trevor on the bench. He watched Steve return to the bench where he and Rob were taking turns. Pretty cool, he mused. When Steve first joined their group, he would have had trouble picking up that dumbbell with both hands. Now the guy was bench pressing one-hundred-fifty pounds.

When Steve finished his set of overhead presses, he turned toward Trevor. "Hey, Trevor, thanks again for helping out with getting Rob to his horse therapy."

"No problem. I'm looking forward to it." Spending summers at his grandparents' farm growing up back East, he'd enjoyed caring for their horses. But after he'd lost his legs in the war, he'd let go of that world completely.

A light blanket of melancholy settled over him, as distant memories of *before* pushed through his thinking. So long ago, you'd think that it would no longer bother him.

LATER THAT WEEK, KRISTY STOOD IN THE CENTER OF the smaller ring, lunging Sugar—working the horse in a circle around herself. The horse trotted along kicking up damp sand here and there. Sugar had a really nice attitude toward her work. She was silly and a prankster when out in the pasture with the other horses. But when she came into the ring, she took things seriously.

Rob and Sugar worked really well together. Made a great team.

Sugar hadn't been worked much in the last couple of days, so Kristy wanted to get her nicely warmed up and allow her to blow off some of her excess energy before she and Rob started their session.

After ten minutes of going at a strong trot, Kristy encouraged Sugar to an easy canter, her hoof beats and breathing creating a pleasant rhythmic cadence. The horse had cantered around the ring four times, when Kristy's attention was pulled from her task.

"Ho," she murmured softly, slowing Sugar to a walk.

The sound of a vehicle coming up her drive became clearer as it neared. An impressive dark blue van with striking black detailing pulled slowly into view. It looked just like those fancy conversion vans from her youth. Beautifully restored, too. The vehicle made its way over to the ring and parked under the largest of her five massive cottonwoods.

Rob jumped out as soon as the passenger door flew open.

"Hey Rob," she called over.

He waved and jogged over to the rail of the ring. Sugar being as crazy about Rob as she was, walked over to him. When reaching the pipe fence, she lipped at the shoulder of his green T-shirt. He ducked through the pipe fencing and reached up, patting Sugar on the neck.

Kristy dropped the whip and commenced to winding the lunge line in a circle between her open palm and elbow, while walking toward them.

She was so proud of Rob and how far he'd come. When he'd started with her a couple years ago, she'd had to work on getting him to come within twenty feet of any of her horses. When he came for his very first session, she'd had a hard time even getting him out of the car.

"Ok, Rob. Take Sugar over to the cross-ties. Time for you to get her ready to ride." She unclipped the lunge line and flipped the reins over the horse's head, handing them to Rob.

"I'm on it, Kristy." He took the reins, his right hand closer to the bit, the slack in his left. "Come on, Sugar." She followed him dutifully. When he reached the crosstie bays, he put a halter over Sugar's bridle and snapped the ties to each side. Then he disappeared into the tack room only for a moment and came out with a brush and curry comb, going straight to work grooming Sugar.

Stepping through the pipe fence, Kristy walked closer to the van, then waited. The clunk of the back doors of the van opening caught her attention, then the gears of a ramp engaged. This Trevor guy had a sweet set up. The angle of the vehicle and open back door of the van shielded him from view. When he cruised the all-terrain wheelchair around, moving toward her, her eyes grew wide, and she found herself stunned to silence.

Rob's good Samaritan was the guy from the store and, dear Lord, he looked even better than he had the first time.

When he gazed up into her face, she noticed his amused smile of recognition. He was one of those people who, when they smiled, it reached all the way up to the crinkles of their eyes. In his case, huge hazel eyes. Then it reached all the way down to the dimples on his clean-shaven cheeks. His gaze sparkled with mischief, before he looked down at the terrain he negotiated.

The guy beamed vitality.

Something she wanted, really wanted.

Ever since Brad left her high and dry last year, for a younger model, it had taken a bit of the starch out of her. Ok, a lot of starch.

That kind of thing had never happened to her before and her confidence in herself as a desirable woman had pretty much bit the dust. Luckily, she'd only run into Brad and Amber once in public. That was back in June, at Save-in-Store buying windshield-wiper fluid.

It had been pretty awful. She'd just come from a show and smelled like horse. Her hair had been in the messiest of pony-tails. She'd had dirt on her face, which she hadn't realized until she'd gotten home.

Brad and Amber had looked fantastic. They both radiated that healthy glow of just coming from a workout. Amber wore short-shorts and a crop top, and damn her, she did them total justice.

At fifty-eight, Kristy took pride in keeping herself in decent shape. But Amber was somewhere in her thirties, and there was just no comparison. She felt herself flush with embarrassment at the memory of it.

"What's wrong?" he asked, rolling closer. Trevor's deep voice broke through her haze of humiliation. There was concern in his tone.

"Oh, nothing, really." *Kristy! Get a grip.*

She and Trevor moved easily in tandem, toward where Rob was brushing Sugar. Sunlight streaked through the old cottonwoods, dappling the bark-covered path. They went along in silence, but it wasn't a silence that was at all weird.

The thought of how she'd stalked away from him at the store, like a big goof, made her cringe. Not just cringe but honestly feel awful. Her business was one where she worked around people every day who were often judged harshly, unfairly, and immediately. And in the store, she'd done just that. *Damn!*

"You always this quiet?" he asked, looking up at her with his left eyebrow pulled up.

"Nope, not at all." She crossed her arms under her breasts and looked down. "Just trying to stay focused." *Liar.*

He swung his chair around in front of her, blocking her path, halting her movement. Sitting back, he looked up into her face. And there went that total-face smile again. *Radiant!* She found her lips forming a smile back all on their own. Her stomach did a soft little somersault.

"Better."

What was she doing? Getting all moony over a total stranger.

Trevor leaned back in his chair. "You're getting that look again."

She chuckled.

Rob and Sugar had stepped back into the middle of the ring, all tacked up and ready to go. He even had his helmet and vest on.

Aggie had trotted up and sat next to Trevor. Baxter offered his growly bark thing from over on the porch.

"Rob, take Sugar into the ring and let's get started."

TREVOR ROLLED OVER TO THE PIPE FENCING surrounding the ring that Rob, Sugar, and Kristy had just closed themselves into.

He leaned over and rested his arms on the middle rung of the pipe fencing, watching the session progress. It was so cool seeing Rob engaged in another sport and killing it. His mastery of the situation was apparent. Confidence spilling out all over the place. Trevor smiled.

He and Rob had been hanging at the gym for over a year now and he'd never mentioned that he was involved with horses.

It was nice being around them again.

Relaxing back in his chair he noticed that he'd acquired a companion. Someone must have gotten loose from their stall. From behind him the horse gave a couple loud snorts, then pawed anxiously at the ground.

"Don't move," Kristy said low, her tone serious, her big blue eyes wide with concern. "Houdini!"

Trevor slowly turned his chair to face the horse. A huge gray gelding stood very close to him. With wide eyes, he tossed his head around, then suddenly he reared up and stood on his back legs for what seemed like ages.

He had seen this kind of behavior from males all his life, and he'd tired of the bullshit posturing crap decades ago. Trevor didn't move, didn't budge or flinch. He just stared the horse in the eye and sat back, waiting for the guy to finish his display.

When the horse dropped down from rearing, he stood still, looking slightly unsure.

Trevor pivoted his chair back toward the ring to continue watching the activity there, ignoring the big guy.

He registered the sound of the horse slowly stepping up beside him. Trevor continued to ignore him. The horse's warm breath fanned the side of his neck, then the weight of a muzzle rested on his shoulder. He scooted away from the contact. The horse followed, seeking out Trevor's shoulder once more. He scooted away again. When the horse tried the third time, Trevor turned to him. They were nose to nose. In a loud, stern voice he said, "Quit!" The horse pulled his head up, remaining motionless, then turned to look over at Kristy, Rob, and Sugar like he wasn't sure what to do next.

"Take it easy," Trevor murmured to the horse. The animal looked at him then eased his haunches down, sitting like a dog, right next to his chair.

Trevor looked out into the ring to see Kristy and Rob standing stock still, staring at the two of them. They both looked like they'd seen a marvel of nature.

"What?" he demanded. Houdini threw his head up and down a few times in apparent agreement.

———

AFTER ROB'S RIDE, KRISTY INVITED THE TWO OF them to her covered patio for some lemonade. Nice, because it was still getting damn hot for October. Double nice because he'd get to spend more time in the company of this fascinating woman.

The fact that her entire place appeared to be accessible was rare and more than wonderful. Both front and back doors were wide and appropriately ramped.

During his time in Nam, he'd become hyper aware of his surroundings. That vigilance had never left him after he got back. Maybe eased up a little though, over the years. Always checking to see how he'd need to negotiate his environment. From safety monitoring, to the need to find a place to sneak off to take a whiz.

He didn't mind getting assistance with his chair being pulled up a step or two, to gain access to someone's home. But often a person's place was totally *not* situated for a set of wheels, and the whole process usually made the person living there noticeably uneasy. Nope, he wouldn't have to worry about that here, he thought, smiling to himself.

"Would you like some more lemonade, Trevor?"

Kristy's question broke through his musings. He held out his glass, and she topped it up.

"You know, I've never seen Houdini respond to a man like that. He was a cow horse for about five years before I got him, and by the looks of the gall marks on his back when he got here, he'd had a hard life on that ranch."

He grinned at the memory of the trouble she'd had getting that horse into the small ring after Rob's session. Seemed like the big guy didn't want to leave his side. Then, once she'd gotten him secured there, Houdini had lipped at the bolt for a good five minutes trying to get back out. Only this time, she'd secured it with a bull snap as well, so he wasn't going anywhere.

"From the way you responded to him, I'm thinking you've spent some time around horses," she said.

He nodded. "Summers at my grandparents' farm growing up. After I came back from Nam that all stopped, of course."

Trevor leaned back in his chair. He didn't want to go any further into that subject with her, or anyone for that matter.

"Can I use your restroom?" he asked.

"Of course." She stood, then led him through the patio door, and into her home. The décor was warm and interesting without being too showy, or girly. They passed by a bookcase with framed photographs. He stopped and picked one up to get a better look.

In the picture, Kristy, in her early twenties maybe, rode a horse bareback. The shot caught them both, as the horse jumped a fallen log. She wore cutoffs and a red tank top. Her long blond hair flying all around her.

"This is a great shot."

"Long ago and far away." She grinned at him. "Reminds me of when I was fearless, and to keep trying to think that way."

He pivoted his chair toward her. "You haven't changed much."

She looked down at the floor, blushing.

Oh man, this gal's easy.

"The bathroom is this way," she said, walking on ahead of him. She stopped, motioning to a wide-open doorway. Had to be close to thirty inches wide and dear God, the door was recessed. How great was that?

"Thanks," he murmured.

Turning, she stepped away toward the back of the house.

As he rolled inside, in awe, his gaze met the ultimate adapted bathroom.

I'm in love.

The sink was a roll-under. Beside the toilet stood an ultra-modern bar for support. Looked more like a sculpture.

But the roll-in shower was the real showstopper. It ran wall-to-wall, spanning the whole back of the room. He couldn't help imagining himself sitting on that bench naked, with Kristy equally naked sitting on his lap. *Oh, man!*

"You alright in there, Trev?" Rob's voice sounded through the door. "You've been in there a while."

Trevor laughed. "Yep, I'm good. I'll be out in a minute."

TREVER PULLED HIS VAN UP IN FRONT OF ROB'S house, in the shade of a dense row of ash trees.

Rob made no move to get out. He sat looking ahead through the windshield, his jaw set tight.

He turned toward the kid. "What's up, dude?"

Still looking ahead. "Kristy is a really, really nice lady."

"She is," he said nodding, wondering where this was going.

"She was real sad for a long time when that rat bastard left her for another lady."

"That happens sometimes, Rob, and it's hard." The guy didn't swear very often, so this must be big to him. Looked like the kid was her champion and he wasn't done.

"Rat bastard's new lady looks a lot like my cousin Laurie."

Holy crap, he'd met Laurie at the gym, and she was like, thirty, maybe. *Ouch.*

"I saw the way you were looking at her." Rob looked down for a moment, then up, then back at him, right in the eye. Warning and maybe a little disapproval in his gaze. "Like she was a big giant chocolate ice cream cone, or something."

Trevor sat up straight, feeling his brows lift all on their own.

"So, if you're going to try to be her boyfriend, you better treat her nice!"

He didn't really know how to respond to that. Sure, he'd had a few fantasies about the woman, who wouldn't? But really, after Carrie? No go.

"Rob, I think she's a very nice lady, and she's very nice to look at, too. But I hadn't thought of what you're talking about."

"Well... watch yourself. Ok?" Rob looked back down in his lap, like maybe he'd gone too far.

Trevor bit his bottom lip to keep himself from grinning his ass off. "I will, I promise."

Trevor chuckled as he watched Rob clear the steps and walk into his house.

He sat for a moment, gripping the steering wheel. He'd always appreciated eyeballing a fine-looking woman. But this was more than eyeballing. This one seemed to be getting into his head. Showing up in his thinking at the strangest times. That hadn't happened with anyone since Carrie died.

He'd been alone with his thoughts and memories of Carrie for four years now. Hadn't had sex for longer than that because she'd been so sick for more than a year before she died.

Why, suddenly, did he want to get *this* woman alone and naked?

Guilt stomped all over his thinking, causing him to read-just himself in his chair.

He turned over the engine and put the van in gear, securing his grip on the push/pull to his left. Rolling forward, he cleared his head thinking of the stuff he needed to get done today. Needed to hit the store, stop over at Marshall's place and pick up his titanium chair. It had needed a tune-up for a while. Then he'd fit in a workout at the gym before dinner. Today was quad and glute day.

Currently he was working on bulking up. Then at the end of the month he'd go on prep for the ABQ Open. Body-building competitions were such a challenge. All that training helped him keep his aging joints limber, maintain muscle tone, and optimize circulation, something amputees needed to keep in mind. Bodybuilding also helped him stay focused and helped keep his grief at a tolerable level.

Trevor pulled up into the driveway of his ground-floor condo, with thoughts of Kristy again tightening his guts.

Tossing his keys onto the coffee table, he looked at the

considerable display of pictures of Carrie arranged on the big white bookcase against the back wall of his living room.

Sitting back in his chair, taking in all the pictures and mementos, he realized the bookcase was a veritable shrine to her. He wondered what Kristy would think of his shrine.

As he rolled back to his bedroom the image of Kristy, naked, sitting on that teak bench in her shower jumped into his mind, again.

No!

CHAPTER 3

The next morning Kristy sat on her back patio drinking her beloved mocha coffee, heavy on the milk, thank you.

She watched the horses munch their breakfast in peace, while the sun climbed steadily over the cottonwoods. She loved seeing this, loved seeing them together out there, taking their ease while enjoying their alfalfa. It was a meditation of sorts.

She needed that. Because ever since she'd run into Trevor at the Nature Mart store, her peace had been disturbed.

Kristy cough-growled and picked up her coffee cup, holding it up in front of her chin. She leaned over to feel the coffee's steam moisten her morning dry eyes.

No clients were scheduled for that morning. She toyed with different ways she could spend her day. There were always more barn chores to be done, but that didn't set right with her current mood. Something else. She let her mind wander. She hadn't been to the Grower's Market in downtown Albuquerque in forever.

Yeah, she'd do that.

She fed Baxter and Agnes, and did her double check of the closures on the pasture. Didn't want Houdini setting himself and everyone else loose for a hay-day while she was gone.

After showering she took a little more time picking out her clothes, and doing her hair and face, than she had in quite a while.

What's up with that?

KRISTY PULLED HER TRUCK INTO A SMALLER-THAN-was-wise space in the street behind Robinson Park. Parking was a premium at this deal unless you were there before eight o'clock. She squeezed out of her vehicle with serious care, as there wasn't more than ten inches to move without hitting the silver Porsche next to her.

She secured her red backpack over her shoulders and headed on into the market. The crisp fall-morning weather enhanced her buoyancy. Horse work was most enjoyable in the fall—for her anyway. She realized her mood was sneaking up into the optimistic level, with a chance at joy. That was new. *Wow!*

She stepped along the rows of booths, checking out the many goods. *Ooh!* On the way back to the car she really needed to stop at the La Yum tent for one of those amazing-looking chocolate eclairs.

Her walk took her here and there, up and down the rows of booths. Colorful and interesting items sparked her curiosity. She checked out a horse pendant at one of the jewelers. As she picked it up to get a closer look at its abstract design, she heard someone calling her name.

Caught up in a hazy mist of confusion, she looked in the direction of the voice to see Rob, Trevor, and another big and rather fearsome-looking guy sitting behind the table of the ABQ Vets Network.

Rob waved her over. She smiled to him and stepped up to the booth.

"Hey, Rob."

"Hi Kristy."

Trevor waved, smiled his full-face smile. "Kristy, this is Mike," he said, motioning to the scary one. Mike's face split into a huge grin, totally changing fearsome to friendly. He nodded to her, then looked over to Trevor and lifted an eyebrow.

Trevor cleared his throat. "What brings you out this fine fall morning?"

"Oh, a clear schedule and an impulse to do something different today."

"How long has it been since you've been to the market?"

"A couple years, I think."

"We're here at least once a month." He paused. "Have you ever tried the eclairs from La Yum?"

"No, I haven't. But I certainly noticed them walking in."

Mike cleared his throat. "Rob and I have got this if you and Kristy want to tour around."

Trevor nodded to Mike. "Well then, let's head that way. I'm in need of some frivolous carbs," he said winking. He'd remembered what she said when she'd been flirting with him at Nature Mart. *Had I really been flirting? I don't flirt.*

"OK, lead the way."

Trevor backed up his sleek titanium chair and rolled around Rob and the table, pulling right up next to her. He had on well-worn black sweats that looked like they'd been cut off and expertly sewn up about two inches passed his stumps. Along with the sweats, he'd donned a maroon hoodie. That hoodie was filled out quite nicely about the chest, arms and shoulders. *Oh, my.*

"You are going to love these," he said, grinning with enthusiasm.

They moved along one of the paths until the aroma of cinnamon made her mouth water. Trevor pulled up to the booth's counter.

"We'd like a couple of your eclairs."

Kristy got a closer looked at the eclairs lying in a rectangular pan, on a table at the back of the booth. *Oh. My God.* Those things are as big as a small loaf of bread.

"Whoa," she put up her hand, "You mind if we split one? I don't want to be in a carb coma the rest of the day."

Trevor laughed and nodded. "Smart." He turned to the vendor, "*One* of your eclairs, Ernie."

"Sure thing, Trevor." The guy behind the booth turned away from them. When he turned back to them, he held out an eclair, that covered the entire paper tray it sat on. Holy crap, if she ate her entire half—that would be it for lunch right there. Her heart melted at the thought of Trevor not having a care about her eating an entire one of those. Brad would have warned her that it would be a threat to her waistline. *Jerk!*

Trevor held their prize while he wheeled one-handed to the empty bench about thirty feet from the action. As she followed him, he parked himself at the left side of the bench.

When she sat down next to him, he handed her their treasure, and she sat it on her lap.

"Dig in," he said, tearing off a nice chunk of the end closest to him, and devouring it. She followed suit and, dear Lord, he wasn't exaggerating. The pastry was delicious, perfect. She hadn't planned to, but she moaned out loud.

Trevor chuckled.

When they were about three-fourths done with the eclair, the feeding frenzy abated. Kristy sat back and took a long slow breath. Stretched out her neck, noticing that a pleasant calm had descended upon her. And that she was overcome with a lovely sense of satiation.

The right side of Trevor's mouth turned up, and he leaned in. "I know. Feels like you just had sex, right?"

That made her cough and laugh at the same time. "Probably the closest thing to it, at least for me for quite a while." She couldn't believe she was self-disclosing like this. It's just that for some reason she found herself nicely comfortable around this man.

"Me too." He looked down and braced his hands on his stumps. "My wife died four years ago." She looked over at him, and his eyes were big, like he'd surprised himself by what he'd said.

"I'm so sorry," she said reaching over without thinking, placing her open palm on one of his hands.

"Thank you."

Well, that was sure a conversation changer. She felt like she needed to add her situation to it, to kind of balance things out. "Last year, my fiancé left me for a younger woman."

Trevor placed his other hand on top of hers. When she turned to him, his gaze was fierce. "He was a damn fool."

"In hindsight, he did me a favor, but at the time it was a total confidence killer."

"I can imagine."

"Hey, Trevor," Mike came striding over. "I've got to get home and take over with Sophie. Viv has an impromptu nurse meeting at the hospital."

Trevor leaned back in his chair. "Ok, you go on. I'll head back right now. Rob will be fine until we get back over there."

"Ok, man. I'll see you at the gym tomorrow."

"Sounds good."

Mike turned his attention toward her, and smiled. "Nice meeting you, Kristy."

"You too," she said.

Kristy stood as Mike walked on. She and Trevor strolled back to their booth. Rob was standing there, talking with great confidence to a man, holding out a pamphlet to him.

"It's so nice to learn about all these different facets of Rob's world. He's blossomed amazingly over the last couple years," she said.

"Would love to think we had a small hand in that," Trevor said grinning. "About a year ago Mike and I came upon him at the gym just as a small group of idiots were giving him a hard time. We invited him to work out with us, and he's been a part of our little team ever since. His community support guy, Steve, is working out with us now, too."

"Ah, so that's how you know Steve."

"Yeah. Both have made huge gains with their fitness."

"You sound like a coach or a gym teacher."

He laughed. "I feel like one sometimes. You know, Mike is at UNM, studying to become an adaptive PE teacher."

"Really? I remember toying with that idea when I was in college. Nothing like being able to go to work in your sweats every day."

"Right?"

As they approached the Vet's Network booth, Rob was in rare form. Being all social and helpful with people who'd approached. She was so proud.

Trevor rolled around the table, taking his original spot behind it. Addressing her, he held out a flyer and said, "Ma'am, might I interest you in the upcoming VFW fundraiser? Live music, taco bar ...me," he said with a confident grin. He wrote his number on the flyer and handed it to her.

Was he asking her out on a date? For real? Kristy froze.

She wasn't sure how she felt about that, she wondered as she stuffed the flyer into her backpack. At this point, her life was her own. Loud or quiet, asleep or awake. Everything on her own terms. She'd given up a lot of that with Brad. Did she really want to dance near that flame again? "I don't know, Trevor. I need to check my work schedule."

He sat back in his chair, cocked his head and one eyebrow lifted in disbelief. "You work on weekend evenings?"

"Well ...no." So embarrassing. She looked over at Rob, his face scrunched up in a disapproving look, as he backed further into the tent.

"I might be interested," she said, her voice strangely hoarse.

She needed to make a quick exit. This situation was getting entirely too real, too fast. "See you guys," as she practically ran out of the park.

When she got home, she took her recently way-more-used cell phone out of her backpack and texted Trevor. "Yes, I'll go."

CHAPTER 4

Kristy passed the basket of tortillas to her right, to her buddy Mattie, then held up her glass of extremely dry red wine, proposing a toast to the whole group.

"To us, and these ongoing gatherings of kindred spirits! So great to see everyone!"

Clinking glasses and sounds of agreement filled the air around their table at Ole's, their favorite eatery to meet up for what they'd dubbed the Mostly OT Women's Round Table. They'd been gathering socially since the original three members met in OT school. Additional members had been adopted along the way.

Ruth piped up from across the table, giving Kristy an analytical grin. "You're looking spunkier than you have in a while. What have you been up to?" She sat back, studying Kristy further, then leaned in as to focus harder. "You met someone, didn't you?"

Kristy put herself right in their crosshairs by blushing painfully. Hot and prickly, that heat shot straight up her cheeks.

Pandemonium exploded around the table, while Kristy attempted to sink into her chair.

"Spill, spill!" demanded Mattie.

"There's nothing to spill."

All her friends went instantly silent, still as statues—staring, waiting ...waiting.

Oh, God this is embarrassing. "I have a date this Saturday night."

Conversation exploded again.

"More intel!" demanded Raquel, sitting to her left.

"He's not another gym-rat, is he?" asked Patty.

"Well, yeah," she responded.

Groans all around.

"Actually, he's a Bonafide competitive bodybuilder," she reported, with a sense of pride that surprised her. Unlike her wanna-be ex.

"What's his name?" demanded Raquel.

"Trevor Drury."

"I know that guy," said Ruth. "Before he retired, I made several referrals to him over at DVR." With her elbow on the table, Ruth dropped her chin on her hand, a ponderous expression covering her face. "I've never had sex with a guy with no legs. Perfect opportunity to do tops. You'll have to tell us all about it," she said, dipping a chip into queso.

Raquel gasped. "Ruth, I can't believe you just said that!"

"My thinking hasn't gone that far forward," mumbled Kristy.

"Liar," responded Ruth, crunching.

Thank heavens for the only social worker at the table, and her ability to change the course of a conversation in a nanosecond. "What do you and Trevor have planned?" asked Lucy.

"Some deal put on by the VFW. Trevor's a Vietnam Vet. Sounds like he's pretty involved with veterans' activities. He mentioned something about dinner and dancing."

"He's *way* involved, and he's a good guy, Kristy," assured Lucy. "I know him, too. He's good friends with my brother-in-law, Mike. They are gym buddies."

"You know how guys in chairs dance, right?" Ruth grinned, nodding. "You get to sit on his lap for the slow songs."

Kristy leaned forward, attempting to be serious. "To be really honest, I just want to get to know him better as another human on the planet."

"Riigghht, with all that muscle and endurance, you just want to talk."

"Ruth! Enough!" said Patty. She turned to Kristy. "Wait, Vietnam? Doesn't that make him a *bit* older than you?"

"I don't know how old he is. We haven't talked about that. I'll tell you one thing. He may be older, but he makes my ex look like the classic scrawny guy at the beach."

Her tablemates all shut up at that, as the waitress put down hot plates all around the table.

"We all hope you have a great time, Kristy. You deserve it," said Lucy, as they all tucked in to their dinners.

LATER THAT WEEK, TREVOR LOWERED THE LIFT OF his van to the ground in front of the haircutting place Mike had referred him to. Mike had remarked that his last haircut looked like something you'd get from the barber on base. Probably looked that way, because he had gotten it cut by an old barber who used to work on base.

He knew he was looking shaggy. Had enjoyed his long-haired days after Nam and had been toying with the idea of growing it longer again. Somehow after meeting Kristy, that idea had lost its appeal. He wanted to make a good impression, so a haircut was definitely in order before their date tomorrow.

Christ, a date. Was he really ready for this? He exhaled slow.

He cruised on into Clips, Cuts & Spa, noting that it was one of those modern places with all the chrome and black décor. The type of place he'd always avoided. Feeling totally fish-out-of-water, he rolled up to the counter, which was thankfully waist-high to a walking person.

It was always better, when he didn't have to peek up over a high countertop like a five-year-old, as happened on regular occasions.

The woman behind the counter spied him. "Oh, hi! I'm Katie," she said smiling. "You must be Trevor."

He leaned back in his chair, a vague sense of warning traveling up his spine. He rolled backward a couple feet. "I am."

"When Mike called, he described you." She smiled big and genuine. "He also set you up for the Men's Special."

Oh, shit. That didn't sound good at all. "I'm just here for a haircut."

"Of course, you're getting a haircut, along with some of our other top-notch services. Mike already paid for the whole thing."

That sneaky bastard. "Like... what other kinds of services?" he asked, backing up another foot.

"You'll see. Come on back."

When they reached her station, before she said anything, he pulled up next to her chair, locked his wheels and transferred neatly up into her chair. Her eyebrows rose in amazement.

He did have a great deal of upper body strength, and could easily maneuver himself around, in such a way that he wouldn't be able to if he had legs. Most people don't really flash on how heavy legs are.

"Here, let me take your jacket."

He pulled it from his shoulders and handed it to her. Then she draped it over the back of his chair.

The expression on her face was one of focus, contemplation. "How do you usually wear your hair?" she asked, gently raking her fingers through the hair at the top of his head.

"Short, like a high-and-tight."

"You know, there are styles fashioned along the lines of a high-and-tight, but with a little more on top and some other stuff going on around the sides. With all these nice waves, I really think that would look good on you."

Maybe it was time to try something new, he thought, exhaling. "Ok, but don't leave me looking like some goofy old hipster."

Katie laughed at that. "No worries. I'll take good care of you."

He turned, looking up into her eyes. "You'd better."

She laughed again.

He liked this gal. She wasn't at all affected by his reticence, or his missing legs.

"So today you are scheduled for an anti-aging hot towel facial, a manicure, and a sports massage. And the haircut, of course. Marie will start with your manicure, then the facial with Suz, the massage with Cathy, and then the cut with me."

He'd been stuck in some limiting ruts, as happens a lot when one is over sixty. It was time to shake things up a little.

"Ok, I'm in."

He transferred back into his chair, and she led him over to where the manicurists were.

"Hi, I'm Marie."

He smiled and nodded.

She reached out toward him, confusing him at first. Then flashing, he placed his hands on the table of her station.

She grasped both of his hands and inspected them,

turning them over and back. "You want me to do anything about these calluses, or should I leave them alone?"

"I'll keep them, thanks." They were a protection lifting. And he didn't want to part with them, he'd earned them, damn it.

"No problem. But, you know, they can be kind of scratchy when you're touching someone," she said, giving him a wry smile.

Well, hell. He hadn't thought of that. Not that he'd imagined he'd get anywhere near second base with Kristy on their first date. The idea of causing her any kind of discomfort irritated him. The fact that he worried about that irritated him.

"How about this?" Marie said, tracing his callus with her fingertip, "We can get rid of these rough edges and just soften them up."

"Yeah sure, let's go for that." Big old conflict, even thinking about getting close to another woman, when Carrie still held such a big place in his heart and soul.

Man, how things change when one got older. When he was in his thirties, a date was pretty much synonymous with getting laid. Women's curiosity about his abilities, in view of his disability, had worked out well for him in that arena.

Now that he was older, things weren't that simple. He really liked the idea of having sex again, but what would a woman expect of him other than the indoor sports? Commitment?

"Earth to Trevor?" Marie was grinning at him. "You certainly went somewhere else." She chuckled. "And I can guess where."

AS TREVOR ROLLED INTO HIS PLACE, HE THREW HIS keys in the green glass bowl on the table by the door. As he did, he realized that despite his generalized arthritis and other age-related annoyances, he was feeling damn good physically.

Holy shit, that massage! He hadn't had that much physical attention from a woman since way before Carrie died. Honestly, it felt so damn good to have a woman's hands on him. He'd been a little nervous that he'd get a hard-on during that massage. *Close, but no cigar.* He chuckled to himself.

He looked at his hands. They looked really nice. Not a hard spot that would snag delicate skin. Unbidden desire surged through him at the thought of touching Kristy's bare skin. Such a rush of feeling regarding another woman spurred doubt and guilt. Like he was cheating or something.

He checked himself out in the mirror by the door. His hair looked great. Running his fingers through his new do, he thought of when Katie had covered his hair with that purple goo, and he'd freaked out a little. She promised him, she was indeed *not* coloring his hair, but that the purple stuff would make his colors really pop. But damn, if that stuff hadn't highlighted the white and silver, just like she said it would.

He looked to the sides of his head, at both ears. *Ha!* No more hair sneaking out of his ears. *Yes!* Out of all the wonderful trappings paired with getting older, the ear hair thing was one of his least favorite.

He remembered he needed to get the couple of products he'd been talked into buying out of the van. Boy, would the guys in his Vets group get a big kick out of that?

He rolled over to the couch and locked his chair, then transferred onto his couch. Yanking up the remote, he went to YouTube and poked around. What was the fancy name for what Kristy did... hippo? therapy? He did a search and learned there was a ton of vids on the subject. If he was going to spend some time with that woman, he should probably get a little more acquainted with her work.

Before meeting her, he didn't even know that what she did was a thing. The more vids he watched the more fascinated he became. What an amazingly interesting and worthwhile profession.

CHAPTER 5

L ooking into the mirror, Kristy held several different tops up in front of her, trying to decide which would be the best for the fundraiser. She went with a red-and-black paneled tunic, with a round neck. It made her middle look slimmer, and her torso look longer. Nothing like the onset of "mental-pause" to start the unfortunate thickening of a gal's mid-section.

She'd pair it with some stretchy black jeans and booties. *Yeah, that'll work.*

Standing in front of the bathroom mirror, she removed the few large hot rollers she'd placed here and there for a bit of lift. She was the only one she knew who even owned a set of them anymore. But she had skills in that area and not in the use of those straighteners. Why go to a straightener, which seemed like an oxymoron anyway, to *curl* her hair when she had the know-how with something she already had. Right?

She nodded to herself and put her rollers back in the bathroom cabinet. Then attended to a little-more-than-usual in the face painting department, ending up with a lip color of a soft brownish pink. There. Good. OK.

Dear Lord, a date. How can I feel like a dang nervous teenager at fifty-eight? She took a long, slow calming breath.

She fluffed her hair and went out to the living room to wait for Trevor. He'd insisted on driving all the way to Bosque Farms to pick her up, which was about twenty miles south of Albuquerque. He lived in the University area, so it wasn't too far from his place to the south end of town.

Baxter let out one of his lazy woofs, and Aggie stood and joined in with a few staccato barks.

Ah, her date had arrived. She'd left the gate open for him.

She shushed her dogs and opened the door. Trevor had pulled up in front of her door and was almost to the ground on the van's lift.

"Oh, I was hoping to catch you before you unloaded." She walked out onto the porch.

"I asked you out, that means I pick you up at your door, and return you to your door," he said as he rolled over to her.

"Alright," she said smiling. "Please come in while I get my things."

"Sure."

He followed her into her living room, stopping at the foyer. Aggie went over to greet and sniff. He scratched her under the chin. Baxter stayed where he was, but woofed hello.

She retrieved her purse and sweater and headed out the door with Trevor following closely behind. *Oh, God, I just know he's looking at my butt.* Of course, he was. Using a chair, his face was right at to her butt level.

"You're looking at my butt, aren't you?" she muttered without thinking.

Trevor laughed softly. "It's quite a lovely view from back here."

"Trevor," she said under her breath, laughing. Once they'd cleared the front door, she locked up. He took her hand as they made their way toward his van.

TREVOR PULLED UP RIGHT IN FRONT OF THE ABQ Central Hotel, taking advantage of the handicapped parking. She'd driven by the place plenty of times but had never been there before.

She waited for Trevor to unload and come around to the passenger side of the vehicle to open her door.

When he did, she looked down at him. Really checked him out, and his efforts to spruce up. The maroon button-down shirt, stretching across his wide chest, really made his eyes pop. Then she focused on his face; he was clean shaven, and he'd gotten a very nice haircut. *Wow!*

"You look fantastic," she blurted out without thinking.

Those beautiful crinkles at the sides of his eyes creased with the split of an amazing smile.

He tilted his chin up just a bit. "Thank you."

They looked at each other in gentle silence for a moment. Neither moved for a nice stretch of time.

Then Trevor cleared his throat. "The guys are already there, holding spots for us."

He rolled back still holding the door open for her. They strolled around the majestic front staircase leading up to the main entrance, took the side entrance instead and rode the elevator up to the main ballroom.

Kristy was taken by the lovely furnishings and appointments of the place. Trevor remained quiet as they negotiated the area.

They entered the ballroom, to behold a sea of eight-person round tops, and a crowd of people milling about the entire expanse of the area. Up toward the front she noticed Trevor's friend Mike, waving with enthusiasm. She pointed Mike out to Trevor, whose view was obstructed by people moving about. They headed for the table. It was full except for two spaces. One chair and an empty space for Trevor to roll under.

A stunning redhead stood up to her full height, probably six feet, and walked over to her. "Hi. I'm Viv. It's so nice to meet you."

Kristy was a little taken aback by the warm and more than enthusiastic welcome. "Hi, I'm Kristy." Viv took her hand and gave it a nice confident shake.

Then Viv went over to Trevor and put her hands on his shoulders. "How the heck are you, T?"

"I'm great, actually," he said, putting one of his hands over hers, then turned around giving her a kind of serious look. "Hey, who's watching my grand-girl? Who's got Sophie?"

Viv laughed, "She's with Fina, of course."

Then Viv broke out her phone and showed Kristy a picture of a beautiful, almost toddler little girl, with black hair, bright green eyes, and a huge, gummed smile.

"She's a doll," said Kristy, wondering what it would have been like to be a mother.

Then she looked up at Viv in awe. "You look like you've never been pregnant," she said eyeing the woman's small waist, totally flat stomach, and amazing overall physique.

"You are my friend for life," she responded, with all seriousness. "I do spend a lot of time at the gym. That's where Mike and I met." Viv looked back her husband. The guy's adoring gaze indicated he was totally besotted.

Viv sat back down next to Mike and introductions circled the table. Steve and Carmen, Ray and his wife, Danni.

"Where's Rob?" asked Trevor.

"He has a date, that fancy prom one of the churches puts on every year. He's taking a gal he met at his water aerobics class," said Mike as he picked up his water glass for a drink.

"Boy, that guy has a totally active social life," said Kristy.

"Tell me about it," chimed in Steve. "That's an activity he

found all on his own. Gets there by himself on the bus, too. Sounds like he's the only guy in the class and is quite the hit with the ladies."

Their conversation was interrupted by sound checks jumping through the sound system. Then the emcee welcomed everyone, thanking them for their support of the ABQ Vets Network and letting them know that dinner would be served soon. A grand New Mexican buffet offering red and green chili enchiladas, tacos, tamales, and all the trimmings.

She turned toward her date. "Would you please allow me to fix you your plate, so you don't have to put up with that herd of turtles?"

He gave her a frustrated look then looked over at the mob assembling. "Alright, I'll get us a drink from the bar while you do that. What would you like?"

She hadn't had a mixed drink in ages. "Hmm, how about a piña colada?"

He grinned at that. "One coconut milkshake coming up."

"Are you making fun of me?"

"No, no," he grabbed her hand and squeezed. Then rolled off to the bar.

She and Viv and the rest of her dining companions made their way to the buffet line. The energy in the room filled her with positive anticipation for an enjoyable evening.

Joining the ever-growing buffet line, she and Viv made small talk about home and work as they single-stepped it forward.

Some random movement from further up the line caught her attention. A young woman had turned around and was waving at her.

"Kristy? Kristy!"

She was so caught up in conversation with Viv that it took her a while to flash on who was beckoning her. It really cleared her head when Brad turned around to see who Amber was waving at. His expression went blank.

Well, this is interesting. She never thought she'd see Brad at a veteran's function. Then she remembered hearing that Amber's father had served.

"What's wrong?" asked Viv.

"What do you mean?"

"You've stopped moving, and you're standing stone still."

"Oh, sorry," she said stepping forward.

"No worries. Tell me."

"My ex and his girlfriend are up ahead of us in line. The waving platinum-blond in the red dress."

Viv leaned out to get a better look. "Oh, no." Pretty amazing how much understanding and support can be communicated in one tiny phrase. She was quiet for a moment, then, "Shall I go kick his ass?"

Kristy laughed, putting her hand on Viv's arm. "Thank you! But no."

"Are you OK?"

"Yeah, I think so. We don't run in the same circles, so I don't have the occasion to see those two very often." She was thrilled and confused about the fact that seeing them really didn't spin her up hardly at all. Nothing like the time she'd encountered them in the hardware store. To be honest, she felt more surprised than anything else.

Kristy grabbed two plates and commenced to fill them with the evening's amazing fare. Juggling them both, while attempting to keep rolled-up tortillas on both plates, was a bit of a challenge, but she managed to get back to their spot without spillage.

Trevor smiled at her as she approached their table. Her piña colada sat at her place.

"Here you go," she said placing their plates down simultaneously.

"Mmmm, that looks great. Thank you." Trevor lifted his fork but waited for her to sit back down before he hefted a large bite of green chili enchilada into his mouth. The look on his face, akin to sexual gratification.

Whoa.

She lifted her fork along with everyone else and dug in. Trevor was right, delicious.

Everyone around the table must have been hungry, because silence ensued for a good five minutes. Then conversation slowly sprinkled in.

The band had finished setting up while everyone enjoyed their dinner, and slid into a wonderful oldie, "Samba Pa ti" by Santana. One of her favorite slow-dance songs from the old days.

Trevor turned toward her. "Would you like to dance?"

"Why, yes." She took his hand, and they moved out onto the dance floor side by side. When they arrived at a good spot, he stopped and pulled her onto his lap.

"Oh, Trevor, I'm going to squish you," she whispered with embarrassment into his ear.

"Do you have any idea how much weight these stumps of mine can deal with? You're tiny compared to that."

No one had ever referred to her as tiny before. How nice was that!

"As long as you let me know when the blood is squeezed out of them. I'm serious."

"Not going to happen." At that he placed one of her hands on his shoulder and held the other with his. His free hand wheeled them in a slow, small figure-eight.

The warmth of his stumps under her legs was so nice, and having a man's arms around her felt so foreign, and so wonderful. She held onto him a little tighter and he responded in kind, bringing her side up close to his abs.

Brad and Amber danced by, passing behind Trevor. Her dander rose, surprising her.

Without any thought, she planted her mouth on Trevor's, initiating a deep kiss.

He responded with no hesitation, opening his mouth over hers, his tongue gently breeching her lips, exploring.

Kristy's temperature rose instantly, like a hot flash, but in a good way. *Holy shit, I'm kissing a man in public with wild abandon.* Who knew she had that kind of stuff in her anymore?

Trevor pulled back. "I don't know what prompted that, and you know what, I don't care."

She chuckled. "Glad you didn't mind."

"Mind? Woman, my blood's singing halleluiah." He grinned.

Trevor focused deeply on her face. His hazel eyes bright, his lips still wet from their kiss. There was a bit of thickness pressing against her thigh that hadn't been there before that connection.

Hmmm, I guess age wasn't hampering any readiness with this guy. Very nice to know. *OMG, was she really going to jump this guy's bones, or him hers? Or whatever!*

Things were a lot different now that she was older with just a semblance of a waistline. Self-doubt settled in.

Swallowing, she adjusted them both back into dance mode. He took her cue and resumed their figure-eighting. When the song ended, she slid off his lap, then taking his hand they made their way back to their table.

Kristy grabbed her bag, excusing herself to the lady's room. Viv jumped up. "I'll go with."

"They always do that. Why do women go to the head en masse?" inquired Mike, looking semi-mystified.

"You wouldn't understand, my dear," said Viv, kissing the top of his head.

41

They sashayed off together.

When they entered the blue silk appointed restroom, Kristy went to the sink, wet a paper towel and cooled her cheeks with the cold compress.

"What's up?"

"Oh, I don't know. This whole thing is way out of my recent experience."

"Looks like things are going pretty great to me." Viv's enthusiasm was nice.

"I know, I'm just a little worried about what's coming next. He's older than I am and..."

"Oh, you don't need to worry about Trevor. I'm pretty sure his circulation is probably better than mine, with the effort he puts out at the gym," she said, a sweet grin on her face.

She turned to Viv. "I'm not worried about him being able to make it happen. I'm worried about me!" she said putting her palm to her chest. *Why was she telling this stuff to a person she hardly knew?*

"I don't think you need to worry about that either." Viv placed a reassuring hand on her shoulder.

Looking down at the floor, and adjusting her stance, she said, "You don't understand. I haven't... had a first time in over ten years."

Viv bent her head to catch her gaze. "You still don't need to worry. You haven't seen the way Trev looks at you. I have. He's pretty dang entranced."

"Oh, come on."

"Truth! I've known that guy a few years, and I've never once seen him go out with, or even flirt with anyone."

That was encouraging.

She crossed her arms over her chest. "I just don't think I'm ready for the whole... deal... physically. You know?"

"Then don't." Viv grinned and tilted her head. "Nothing like a good old teenage make-out session," she said, winking.

A laugh bubbled up in her. She hadn't thought of that. Might be fun and less intense for now. Taking a full breath, "Ok, we'd better get back or I'm afraid those guys will come in here looking for us."

Viv laughed, too. "You're right about that," she said, linking arms with Kristy. They marched back to the table in tandem.

"It's about damn time, you two. We were about to set out for an extraction mission," said Mike. He took Viv's hand as she sat back down.

Trevor looked up at her with a pleasant smile as she took her seat. He draped his arm around her shoulders and leaned in. "Everything, OK?" he whispered close to her ear.

"Yeah, everything's great."

"Good."

CHAPTER 6

The evening danced along with speeches, announcements, and awards in between musical sets. Kristy hadn't indulged in non-work fun in quite a while. Having such a great time, she realized she'd taken way too long to get back into the social world since Brad left her.

Pondering on him and his ridiculous life choices also made her realize she wasn't nearly as angry about him leaving her as she used to be. There was still a sting, especially at the thought of being replaced by a younger model, but that discomfort hardly held any of her attention anymore. More a response of habit, and it was time to let go of that

She turned to Trevor and found him studying her, with great interest. "What?"

"You're beautiful," he said, his voice low and sandy.

She broke contact with his gaze, looked down, but couldn't help smiling.

"Let's get out of here."

Still smiling, she looked back up into his face. "OK."

Back in Trevor's van, they hit I-25 finding themselves on a pretty much empty stretch of freeway. Nice.

The Jazzmasters' "Peace on Earth" breezed out of Trevor's high-end sound system. Without talking, he yanked the right armrest from his chair and dropped it on the floor behind him. Then he reached over for her hand and placed it on his thigh. Kristy enjoyed the warmth she felt through his gabardine pants.

It was quiet inside the van, no conversation. Both of them seemingly focused on the music.

Kristy was focused all right, on the intriguing man next to her. She couldn't help but sneak repeated glances over at him. Just looking at him made her mouth water. As with most body builders, veins on the arm close to her popped out from the skin in sharp relief. Not to mention the unbelievable definition of his forearms. *Yowzah!* And all of this easily visible with just the light of the dash.

He took a side glance at her, then looked back at the road. "You still hungry? Want me to hit a drive-through once we get off the freeway?"

"No, thank you." She was hungry alright, but not for fast food.

He pulled off on Bosque Farms Boulevard then onto the Loop, then finally through her gates onto her property. He stopped the van in front of her door.

She turned toward Trevor in her seat. "I had a wonderful time. Thank you so much for inviting me," she said, lifting her hand from his stump to take his. "It was great meeting your people, they were all really friendly." She realized that as she'd spoken, she'd leaned closer to him.

Trevor released the chair lockdowns. His grip on her hand tightened as he pushed his ride a little further back. He simultaneously pulled her with a nimble movement onto his lap.

She hesitated, then wound her arm around his shoulders, resting it on the back of his chair.

All motion stopped. Their faces were about six inches

apart. His breath came faster, the warmth of it fanning her face. No time like the present.

She leaned in, gently pressing her lips to Trevor's. The heat of his mouth against hers sent more heat racing through her whole body.

Trevor didn't move, waiting, giving her the lead to their interaction.

Kristy brushed her lips back and forth over his. That sensation tickled her mouth to watering for more. That's when Trevor took over. His arms twined around her, and his mouth opened over hers. Warm and wet, he pressed his tongue inside her and explored.

Without thinking, she responded fully to his ravenous kiss. So, so, good, she thought, wanting to get as close to this man as possible.

With a surge of excitement, she noticed his hand moving from her side to the front of her shirt, making soft passes over her breasts.

More heat shot through her. Skin-on-skin contact would be so nice. Like he'd read her mind, he caressed down the front of her top, then dipped under, traveling back up over her skin. *God, she missed this.*

Trevor's fingertips dipped under the bottom of her bra, bringing it up over her breasts. He didn't hesitate in caressing her, spurring her to kiss him even harder.

He pulled back, and chuckled, but dove right back into that amazing kiss. His kissing her and caressing her breasts triggered long-missed, maybe even a little forgotten, sensations that made her feel younger, so alive and desirable again.

His erection pressed firmly against the right cheek of her rear end. Their breathing came faster.

Oh my God! Too fast. Panting, she pulled back from the wonderful things they were doing and attempted to focus on Trevor's face in the dim porch light. The little she could see was so damn handsome. How could she feel so spectacular and so scared at the same time?

He drew in a deep, full breath and exhaled with a disappointed sigh. "I'm guessing this is good night."

She leaned her cheek against his shoulder. "I'm just not ready for the whole enchilada, not just yet."

He chuckled at that. "I get it," he said as he pulled her bra down to its proper place, and extricated his hand from under her shirt, then kissed her softly on the lips.

"Good night, Kristy."

"Good night, Trevor."

CHAPTER 7

Dropping her hand to rest on Aggie's head, Kristy watched the red taillights of Trevor's van dwindle as he drove away from her house. It suddenly dawned on her how this evening had changed many things. Opened the door to a lot of possibilities. Frightening ones. Unknowns.

By the time his lights finally disappeared, her confidence about the whole situation had dried up like her Mexican sunflowers did at the end of summer.

She put her hand up to her mouth. Her lips were still warm and puffy from his kisses. But fear and wariness had robbed her of that elusive pleasure in an instant. The openness she'd let herself feel for him had just shut tight. It was as if there had never been an open passageway at all.

She walked into her house in a fugue state and lowered herself to the couch, immensely thankful that she'd not allowed things to go any further. And thank God, the interaction had been in the dark. The idea of baring her fifty-eight-year-old torso to someone who looked like they should be on a magazine cover, made her belly contract. What she thinking?

She rose to go back out to do her nighttime check on the horses before going to bed. Walking over to the barn while the dogs did their thing, she made her nightly sweep through the wide passage down the middle of the stall area. They were all laying down but lifted their dozing heads at her approach.

Then she walked out of the barn on the far end and over to Houdini, in his spot in the training ring. He was on his side, completely out, his snoring loud. Really loud. She always wondered if his snoring bugged the other horses. She hated snoring. Brad had been almost as bad a snorer as Houdini. *Wonder if Trevor snores?* Nope, nope. No, she wasn't going there.

She walked back to the house and held the door wide, calling for her dogs. She waited until Aggie and Baxter trundled back into the house and then locked up for the night.

The joy of possibility she'd been harboring this whole week, had faded to a trace. The whole Brad-leaving-her-for-a-younger-woman business rose up in her mind taking a larger place than it had in a long time and squeezing out that tiny bud of joy she'd allowed herself.

The realization was so deflating. *Ugh!* She hated how she allowed someone else's actions to dictate her mood, her feelings, her fears. That sunk her. What a wonderful evening they had together and now all she wanted to do was retreat.

Her returning home early that lovely spring day, to find Brad and Amber naked, entwined on the living room couch, had been devastating.

That *girl* had been boarding her horse with her for about six months. Kristy offered that here and there to help someone out in a pinch. The fact that she was going out of her way to help Amber made it an even more painful betrayal.

Her stomach tightened revisiting all of that. She hadn't really been focused on any of it until just then, after a night with Trevor. Best to pull back right now.

That recognition left her sad and deflated. Staring at the floor, she trudged back to her room to get ready for bed.

TREVOR TOOK THE ENTRANCE TO I-25 RETURNING TO Albuquerque, finding the freeway even quieter than when he'd driven Kristy home. He liked having the road to himself, he mused, as he settled back into his chair. A memory of when he learned to drive a modified vehicle materialized in his head. Laughing out loud at the recollection of taking out a chunk of the neighbor's hedge before he'd gotten the hang of it.

That single memory introduced a flood of recall. His whole reality had changed after stepping on that mine in Vietnam. He'd spent forever at the VA Hospital. During his long convalescence he'd turned into a total asshole who drank too much, picked fights in bars, and got arrested a few times. Negotiating jail in a wheelchair was a huge pain in the ass.

He'd wasted precious years on that anger, his thinking all tied up in what had happened over there, before and after he'd gotten injured.

Then Carrie stepped into his life. She'd come along just in time. She'd been patient with his many struggles but never took any of his shit. He really loved that about her. Something about her—her presence, her laughter, her pretty much instant unconditional love, had spurred him on to want to be a better man.

So, he'd started on that road and his whole life changed. The work was hard, immeasurably hard. It took everything he had. At times he'd felt like he wasn't getting anywhere at all. Carrie had stayed right there, traveling that rough and rocky road with him. They'd spent twenty great years together. Years, that when he thought about them, made his chest ache.

When the diagnosis came, he'd been so sure she'd march

through, and conquer her foe, like she had with pretty much every other challenge she'd faced. The treatments went on and on. But the test results along the way showed the meds just weren't doing their job. Watching her die broke him.

He'd been so into his reminiscing that he almost missed the Gibson exit. His van handled the tight curve of the outlet nicely.

He merged onto Gibson Boulevard contemplating starting this new thing with a woman. His heart sure had some major trepidations about the whole deal, but for the first time his body was in full-speed-ahead mode. It felt odd because he'd never experienced anything like it before.

Crazy, when he thought about getting Kristy in bed, his mouth watered. But his mind was still stuck on high with the loyalty meter.

TREVOR PULLED INTO THE LOT OF KRISTY'S PLACE, parking where he had the last time, in the shade of a large canopy of cottonwoods.

As Rob bounded out of the van, Trevor leaned over to get a look at Kristy before the guy slammed the door. He caught a glimpse of her. She stood, leaning on the fence of her work ring, gazing downward. Not smiling.

"That's not good," he murmured to himself.

He secured the parking brake and unlocked the tie-downs from his chair, swung it around and headed to the back of his van. Pressing the buttons that opened the electric back door and engaged the lift, he wondered what was up with her.

Rolling off the metal platform when it had barely hit the ground, he wheeled over to where she was. Rob had already headed into the barn to get Sugar.

Kristy turned to him, again not smiling. Looking damn

uncomfortable. "I didn't expect to see you with Rob today. Isn't Steve back from vacation?"

"Well, he was keeping it under wraps, until he was sure. But he got a new job, a promotion actually. So, I'll be Rob's transport to therapy until they hire his new community support person."

Her expression tightened.

"What's going on, Kristy? I'm getting something completely different from you than I did last night." Trevor cocked his head.

She stepped back, resting her palms on the pipe fencing, her expression even tighter, totally withdrawn.

Definitely not good.

"I don't think I'm ready for any of this," she said in a low voice, looking down at the backs of her hands.

"You seemed pretty damn ready last night." His tone was a lot sharper than he'd intended. He could feel her withdraw more. *Shit!* He took a breath and tried to relax for a moment, frustrated at the realization of how invested he'd become already. As he rolled toward her a little he asked, "What happened between last night and this morning?"

She turned back toward him, crossing her arms over her chest, squaring off. "I came to my senses. I have no business getting into something with you, or ...or anyone else at this point in my life."

He really felt like lashing out, like being an asshole. Instead, he rolled backward, away from her, pivoted, and headed off toward the pasture where he could see Houdini hanging out by himself.

Aware of his anger, the speed of his wheels was way faster than it should be over the rough terrain. When he reached the pasture, he dropped his hands to his stumps and focused on calming himself down.

A loud nicker came from his left. Trevor looked up to see

the horse stepping toward him. He rolled over to the fence where Houdini stood on the other side. He sat quietly waiting to see what the horse would do. They both waited in silence for a few moments, then Trevor felt the weight of Houdini's muzzle resting on his shoulder. His warm breath was a mild balm to his frustration.

"Well, buddy, your lady over there is trying to give me the brush-off. But having no legs made me develop a stubborn constitution."

Houdini looked over to the ring, where Kristy was closing the gate Rob and Sugar had just passed through. He issued a stout whinny.

That made Trevor laugh.

"She doesn't know me well enough to know what a pigheaded bastard I am." Trevor sat back and grinned to himself as plans of attack began to form in his head. That woman didn't know what she was in for.

He absently reached up to rub Houdini's cheek. The horse raised his head. Trevor looked up at him.

"What's *your* problem?" he asked staring the horse in the eye.

Houdini snorted then, lowered his gray head to Trevor's hand, allowing a cursory pat on the cheek, then pulling away again.

"Jesus, you're both playing hard to get today." Trevor sighed and sat back in his chair.

CHAPTER 8

When Rob had finished his session with Kristy, this time there'd been no offer of lemonade, or hanging out, relaxing on her patio. Just a terse thank you for bringing Rob, and an even terser goodbye.

Boy, her tone and energy were frustrating. Then it hit him, *this* Kristy was more like the woman he'd met at Nature Foods. *Damn it!* What the hell was going on? He was at a totally frustrating loss.

After Trevor dropped Rob off at home, he headed over to the gym. It was back and shoulders day. The place was quiet for late morning. As he returned to the free weight area, he spotted Vivian doing rhythmic curls. He rolled up and waited for her to finish her set.

"Hey, Viv."

"Hey, how are things with Kristy going?" He couldn't miss the optimism in her voice.

"They're not going, out of nowhere. I thought there was a connection. But she's backed away completely, and I don't understand."

Vivian placed her dumbbells on the bench and sat down

on the end facing him. She hesitated for a moment. "I'm not surprised, to be honest. From what I heard about how things ended with her ex, it must have been awful."

"Yeah?"

She hesitated again, studying the callouses on her palms. "She actually caught them together, you know, in the middle of it."

"Oh, God." He shook his head.

"Kristy and Brad were days away from the altar at the time. She had gone to pick up her dress, got home earlier than expected, and found them on the couch, naked."

He sat back in his chair. "Oh, crap! How long ago was this?"

"I think it was a little over a year ago. She threw him out, and got rid of that couch, too. That Brad is a total asshole."

"Sounds like an even bigger fool to me. Well, I guess it makes a lot of sense that she would *not* have a whole lot of trust in men."

"Yeah. Maybe she just needs a little time and space." Viv leaned back and rested her hands on her knees. "I feel weird sharing this, but I think it's important that you know some background here. Especially if you're serious about this. About her."

Trevor nodded. "Thanks, Viv." How serious was he?

Viv stood back up from the bench and continued with her curls.

He went over to get the PVC pipe for his upper body warm up.

Kristy sure hadn't felt at all brittle when they were together last night. *Who knows?*

While transferring and straddling his own bench, he went through his stretches by rote, not thinking at all about the work, but about Kristy. *I guess I am pretty serious.*

He wondered what Carrie would think about that.

KRISTY LED HOUDINI OUT TO THE RING FOR THE morning's first session with Megan. Megan was a tiny little person, with cerebral palsy, but fearless and fun. She was eleven years old, had battled with her mother for a year to let her get on a horse, and finally won. Megan and Rob were probably her most enthusiastic riders.

She really cherished—no, envied—Megan's dauntless courage. Kristy could really use some of that right now. She felt like such a wuss backing away from Trevor the way she had. But whenever she imagined herself letting go of that kind of control again, that total openness she needed to be with him, her heart and gut clamped down on her like she was trapped under one of her horses.

"Kristy, I'm ready to roll," Megan announced, her head bobbing, and smiling big.

So Megan could get closer contact with the horse, she always tacked Houdini up with a bareback pad with stirrups for Megan. Really comfortable for Megan. No problem for Houdini, since she was little and they were only walking.

"Ok. Head up, sit up, hands low. Let's go!" Megan had proper hold on the reins, but Kristy kept the lead rope attached to the bridle and walked her through her session. She stepped forward, and Houdini stepped right along with her. It seemed the smaller, more fragile the person on his back, the more carefully he moved. She loved that about him.

They made one circle of the ring, and she stopped the horse, having Megan drop the reins and stirrups and perform some balance exercises. She extended her arms making small circles, opening and closing her hands. Then did her stretches over the horse's neck, reaching for his ears. She finished with Megan's most favorite movement of them all, laying all the way down on her back stretching her arms above her head, reaching toward Houdini's tail.

Her body movements appeared to quiet the most doing this particular exercise. Kristy spotted Megan the whole time, but her strength and agility had developed to where she barely needed a spotter. For someone who moved all the time, her balance was pretty darn good.

"Ok, Megan, sit back up, gather your reins, find your stirrups. Good, just like that. OK. Would you like to go walking out in the pasture for the rest of our session?"

"Oh, sure!" Her big smile indicated her excitement for the activity.

"Houdini might try to stop and eat grass and you're going to have to keep him moving with your legs and your voice, OK?"

"I can do it!"

"I know you can," said Kristy, nodding her encouragement.

She gave a soft tug on the lead rope and Houdini followed her to the gate, waiting patiently while she opened it and led him through. As they headed into the pasture, Kristy noticed that the grass was in great shape for October, the bare spots from last year filled in. She'd let her little herd out for a nice few hours of lazy grazing later in the day.

Instructing Megan to hold the reins in contact, *she* guided the horse. Kristy held the lead rope lax so Megan could direct Houdini all by herself.

"Where do you want Houdini to go, Megan?" she asked gesturing with her free hand toward the expanse of the acre-large pasture.

"How about to the back where the ditch is? I want to see if there are still any ducks swimming around."

"Great, turn him in that direction and give him a little kick with your heels."

Megan followed the directions and the horse set out at an easy walk toward the back of the pasture. They approached the back fence to the sound of random quacking. Megan's face lit up like sunshine.

Houdini walked right up to the fence putting his head over the top rail, moving till his chest just pressed against the fence.

"Can you see them?"

"A little."

"Grab on to Houdini's mane and stand up way tall in your stirrups. See if that's better."

Megan grabbed on to his thick white mane, and shaking, she stood. "Yes! I see 'em, I see 'em." With bright eyes, she smiled big. "There's five."

She held that pose for a couple of minutes, strengthening her calves, quads and gluts without even realizing it.

Kristy beamed, so happy with what she did for a living. This was pure magic for the rider and the horse.

Something must have startled the ducks. They all took to low flight, flapping away, settling further on down the ditch.

Kristy waited and watched her charge.

Megan sat back down and gave Houdini the signal, pulling back on the reins, backing him up a couple steps from the fence, then turning him back toward the barn. She nudged him with her heels, and he moved forward at a walk that had pep but was easy for Kristy to keep up with.

Bless this guy, she mused. If *she'd* been on his back, he'd be dancing around wanting to gallop back to the barn. She chuckled to herself. Couldn't blame him really, the guy had started his working life out on the track. So, she did on occasion, while riding, she let him have his head and race around the pasture.

When they reached the training ring, Kristy directed Megan to guide him over to the cross-ties area where she would dismount. Megan's mom, Pam, was there waiting for her return. Her expression didn't leave much to the imagination. Megan's dad had dropped her off. She knew her mom would be worried when she'd come to pick up her daughter and she and Kristy were nowhere in sight.

"Mom! It was the best! I rode Houdini all the way over there to the ditch, I guided him by myself and everything."

Her mother's gaze grew large.

Kristy wordlessly held up the lead-rope that was still attached to Houdini's bridle.

"Pam, Megan's skills are strong. She did beautifully." She gave her a reassuring smile then led Houdini over to the mounting block. It was large and wider than the usual so that riders with an unsteady gate or physical weakness could dismount more easily, and on their own. Kristy also had a mounting platform with a ramp and railings, situated beside an opening in the fence of the ring. Megan had expressed early on that she didn't need that much assistance.

The girl dismounted easily and carefully, her mother holding her hand as she descended the three elongated stairs. She turned right around and walked over to Houdini, plastering herself to his chest giving him a big hug.

"Thank you, Houdini, for the wonderful ride," she said, her nose pressed against his chest.

Lowering his head he gently pressed his jaw against her back, hugging her right back.

Megan took a step away from him, leaving her hand on his neck and turned toward Kristy. "I love coming here, thank you too, Kristy."

"You're so welcome."

She and Houdini walked them to their car, waved as they drove off, then she led him over and into the covered cross-tie area. He always stood still for her to untack him. So, there was no need to put him in the ties. She released and pulled the pad from his back. Then she led him over and into the small ring. Slipping the bridle from his head, and the bit from his mouth, she closed the gate. "I'll let you all out into the pasture this afternoon, buddy."

She secured the gate latch, then with the chain, as well. Chuckling to herself, she thought about her escape artist and how much she loved him, and how he drove her nuts sometimes.

She entered the house through the mud room, washing her hands there. When she went into the kitchen, she noticed her answering machine light blinking. Over the last month she'd upped her game somewhat with her cell phone use, and the calls to her landline had slowed down markedly.

Stepping over to the table where the old machine sat, she pushed the button to retrieve her message.

"Hey Kristy, it's me. I want to talk to you about our situation. I need to understand what's going on. Please call me."

"There is nothing going on," she said out loud, cringing the second those words came out of her mouth. *There is no situation.* She sighed as her chest tightened.

CHAPTER 9

"Well, shit," spat Trevor, tossing his cell to the coffee table. He'd left three messages over the last eight hours and zero response from Kristy.

"What the hell is going on?" She sure as shit didn't seem unsure about things when she had her tongue in his mouth.

He grabbed the remote from the coffee table and fired up the TV. Maneuvering over to YouTube, he found one of the videos he'd faved, one of many he'd found, of individuals riding who had no legs.

He really didn't have a huge drive to get back on a horse. But... a plan began to materialize in his mind, and the more play he gave it the clearer and stronger it became. *YES!*

He felt his lips stretching into a big old smile. He knew exactly what he was going to do.

THE SUN HAD SLIPPED GOLDEN BEHIND THE canopies of the cottonwoods, when Kristy stepped into the barn full and ready to engage in at least one of the gazillion barn chores that needed doing. Thank God, the evenings were cooler. This kind of work was a real drag when it was hot. *Ugh.*

She pulled the handles of the wheelbarrow down from where they'd been propped up against the wooden wall and selected one of her three manure forks hanging from that same wall. Laying the fork into the wheelbarrow, she headed over to the first stall. Picking up poop was a necessary reality when you have horses, and she'd managed to turn it into a Zen sort of experience over the years.

The gang was still out in the pasture enjoying their peaceful meander.

She stepped into Stormy's stall and commenced her clean up. It was going to take a little longer than usual because she'd skipped yesterday.

Unaccustomed to the gentle vibration against her right butt cheek, she jumped when her cell phone buzzed. Leaning the fork up against the stall wall, she pulled her phone from her pocket, noting that the call was to her business number. *Trevor!* What was up with him calling her stable number?

Practicing avoidance behavior in one of its purest forms, she waited until the ring ended and he'd left a message. She hesitated, then touched voicemail and listened.

"Hey Kristy, this is Trevor. I'd like to schedule a riding lesson. I can't remember what the rate is, we can deal with that when you get back with me for a date and time. Haven't been on a horse since 1971, and I had legs back then. You have your work cut out for you." He chuckled into the phone, and the sound made her shiver.

"Damn!" No way would she decline. She needed every possible dollar she could make to keep the place going. Not that she was struggling, she was in good shape financially, but that was because she didn't turn down business.

That sneak! He'd found a way to her that she couldn't refuse.

No way was she calling that man right back. She'd finish cleaning up the manure first. Then maybe find something else to do as well. Barn chores never ended.

Making a mental note, she'd have to check the mounting ramp to make sure there wasn't a buildup of leaves, sticks or dirt for his wheelchair to get stuck on. She was sure Trevor was going to want to do as much of this as he could on his own.

Putting her cell back in her pocket, she was hit with a realization she didn't like at all. Why the heck was she carrying her cell around, anyway? That wasn't her thing. Ninety percent of the time her cell lived on her desk right next to her landline and answering machine.

The real reason was difficult to accept. High school remembrance smacked her in the side of the head. Those years when, if she had a crush on a boy, she'd stay within hearing distance of the home phone just *in case* he'd call. *Oh, God!*

She swallowed hard. "Nope! Nope, not happening."

Gripping the fork with renewed vigor, she continued her clean-up work with doubled effort. Lift and dump, lift and dump, lift and dump. Establishing a comfy cadence, she was *not* going to think about the man and how amazingly intriguing he was.

THE NEXT MORNING, TREVOR SAT ON HIS BENCH AT the gym scowling at the look of sheer disbelief covering Mike's face. His response to hearing Trevor outline his new strategy to get up close and personal with Kristy again. Rob's expression was harder to read. It was a little *ha, ha, good luck with that,* and a lot of concern.

"You're going to do what?" Mike replaced two dumbbells back on the rack and stepped over, lowering himself to the bench across from him. Rob stood silent, behind Mike, with his arms crossed tightly over his chest. The silence was totally out of character for the guy. He had a comment for everything.

"I'm going to take a riding lesson, so I can spend more time demonstrating to Kristy that I'm a sincere, worthy and stand-up guy."

"Are you mad? I thought you were pushing it when I first met you, and you told me you were going to compete in body building." Mike leaned closer to Trevor. "With all due respect, bro, you're pushing seventy and you have no legs."

"Yeah, I'm well aware of my age and physical state, Mike," he said with a little more annoyance in his voice than he'd planned. He'd expected a lot more supportive attitude from his friend.

"Sorry," mumbled Mike. "Guess I'm just being a little..." Mike gave him a sheepish smile and looked down, "A little over-protective of Sophie's grandpa."

"No worries. I've been watching a bunch of YouTube videos. There are quite a few legless riders out there."

"No, shit?" Mike leaned back.

"Yep. Hey, I'm not looking to take it up as a regular deal. It's just a way to get closer to Kristy. Besides she's kind of a safety fanatic. You should see how careful and wonderful she is with her riders." He realized he was beaming with pride.

Rob loosened his arms at his chest and jammed them to his sides. "You remember our talk, don't you?"

"I do, Rob, and I will behave accordingly."

The young guy gave him a thoughtful nod.

Mike leaned back putting his hands on his thighs, studying him, like he was looking for something, some change or other. "I've never seen you like this before. Ever."

Trevor felt his face heat up with a blush. *Jesus!* He didn't blush.

Mike issued soft laughter. "Good for you, man."

Time to change the subject. "How's things with your ladies?"

His friend's face morphed into a big infectious smile, "Great as always," he said, grinning.

He sat back remembering a different Mike when they first met a few years ago. A Mike who was not long back from Afghanistan, who was stressed, afraid and furious, and scarily self-destructive. That guy was gone. He still dealt with the backlash of his time over there and would the rest of his life. War never leaves you. With a lot of hard work, Mike was a much happier man now. Markedly more positive, with an easy laugh. Someone who was totally jazzed about embarking on his student teaching next semester.

He finally admitted it to himself. For the first time since Carrie died, he wanted what Mike and Viv had. He really missed having a partner, someone to come home to, someone to laugh with, and plan with. And sex? He missed touching someone and being touched by them. Yeah, he was older, but he wasn't *that* old. Having a sex life again would be great.

Yep, he so hoped this riding lesson would be a re-start of something with Kristy.

CHAPTER 10

Kristy had given him an appointment that following Sunday. He was up, had breakfast and had been decently coffee-ed in plenty of time. He dressed for utility, old jeans, a T-shirt, and a hoodie. Good enough. He sighed, fantasizing for the millionth time how cool it would be to be able to wear boots.

Wheeling out to the garage, he'd use his all-terrain chair again. He'd amassed a small collection of rolling manual transportation over the years. His two favorites were his slick sports wheels and the all-terrain. He transferred from his house chair to the all-terrain and rolled up to the back of his van, then tapped the button on his fob and the back door of the van swung open. He tapped another, engaging the lift. When the lift was down and ready, he rolled on and he was on his way.

Traffic was light from south Albuquerque to Bosque Farms. She'd given him a seven-thirty in the morning appointment thinking she'd irritate him. He chuckled. He was a complete early bird. Seven-thirty was just perfect.

When he got to Kristy's, the gate was already open for him. He pulled in, parked, and unloaded himself.

She had no horse ready, so when he rolled up to her, he asked. "Who am I riding today? I was kind of hoping for Houdini?"

Kristy didn't come any closer to him, so he rolled a little closer to her.

"You know he's not a good fit with men."

Lifting his head to her he said, "That guy and I have an understanding. Besides, you're going to have ahold of him the entire time. Right?"

"Well, yeah." She crossed her arms over her chest. "He could still get nasty."

"I'll take my chances. And really, I'll only be four feet off the ground, right?"

"If you're sure."

He nodded. "Totally."

"Ok then. I'll go get him. You're still going to have to do as much of the prep as possible."

"Yes, ma'am!" he said, grinning. He thought he saw the side of her mouth trying to curve into a smile before she turned away.

Kristy brought Houdini from the small training ring and led him over to the cross-tie area where he was already waiting. The moment the horse saw him he stepped faster toward him, pulling Kristy along with him. When the horse got closer, he slowed and rested his nose on Trevor's right arm, lipping at him gently. Trevor reached up with his other arm and stroked his forehead a few times.

She cleared her throat and placed the bucket of grooming implements on Trevor's lap. "Time to groom your horse. Get to it, mister." Then she attached the cross-ties to Houdini's halter.

He rolled to the horse's side, pulled a curry comb and brush from the bucket before setting it down. With the curry comb he reached down under the horse and rubbed vigorously back and forth between his front legs and back over his belly, where annoying flies liked to hang out and bite.

Houdini grunted and lifted his head up high, his lips shuttering open and closed. That spot was one of the itchiest on a horse, and not at all reachable to scratch. This would set Houdini up for feeling a bit more comfortable while they rode, he hoped. Trevor commenced to brush him properly, noticing that Kristy had taken up the chore on the horse's other side. Nice.

They groomed in silence. Not the most comfortable silence, but they were together in the same space and would be for the next hour or so. *Yes!*

She picked out the horse's feet while he worked on the guy's hind quarters and back legs.

"I think we're good," she said dropping the hoof pick in the bucket. I have both a western and dressage saddle that fit him. I think the western might be more comfortable for you, and you'll have the horn to grab onto in the event of any slippage."

"Western it is," he said, nodding.

Kristy stepped away, heading for the tack shed. He couldn't help watching her butt, her hips sway as she walked. That lovely image got his blood moving faster. He grinned to himself. *Oh, man!*

Just seconds later, Kristy walked out of the tack shed, saddle in her arms. Stepping over to the left side of Houdini she flipped a saddle pad up over his back, then hefted the saddle up onto his back and adjusted it to sit in the right spot, and pushed the cinch off, letting it fall to the other side. Then she pulled it up from under the horse's belly and secured it to her side of the saddle.

"Let me do the bridle."

"Are you sure? He can be a little fiddly about that. He may just put his head up high and refuse to cooperate."

"Let me give it a try."

Kristy handed him the simple snaffle bit bridle, and loosened the halter Houdini wore.

Trevor leaned back and dug into his pocket, bringing out a couple of the handful of sugar cubes he'd stowed there. He'd already learned that this horse would do just about anything for food or treats.

He waved them under Houdini's nose, then lowered his hand to his lap. The moment Houdini lipped the cubes into his mouth, Trevor eased the bit between his teeth and lifted the headpiece up over his ears. Securing the remaining straps, he patted Houdini on the cheek and looked over to Kristy.

She cocked her head and placed her hands on those hips. "That was clever." She grabbed the reins. "Let's hope he stays this cooperative once you get on."

"Are you trying to make this harder? I really don't need that."

Using the reins as a lead rope, she made a clucking sound with her mouth, urging him to a walk.

"See that ramp over there? Roll on over and up. That thing is going to make it so you can mount by yourself." She smiled and he saw sunshine.

Jesus! He cleared his throat and commenced to rolling. When he got closer to the contraption, he couldn't believe he'd not really flashed on what it was before. In the videos he'd watched, he'd seen mostly lifts and extended mounting blocks, like the one over by the cross-tie area.

When he'd gained the platform of the ramp, Kristy already had Houdini standing in place at the inside of the ring, where the fence opened for the platform. His all-terrain chair was a little taller than his others, putting him at a better height to pull himself up on that saddle. He had no trouble pulling himself up on stuff at the gym. He figured he shouldn't have too much trouble getting himself up on Houdini. As long as the horse stood still.

Getting lined up with the horse, he locked the chair and grabbed onto the horn and the back of the saddle.

"Would you hang onto the stirrup on that side?"

"Already got it."

Brilliant minds. Even though his upper-body strength was considerable, to the point where he was confident he'd be able to pull up and throw his right stump over the back of the horse, it was still a bit of a challenge. He managed it okay, but there was nothing at all graceful about the process.

Once he had his butt square in the saddle, Houdini decided they were ready to go, and Trevor had to sit back and grab onto the saddle horn.

"Sorry about that," Kristy murmured, taking a firm grasp on the reins, bringing the horse to a halt.

"I'm good," he said, centering himself up again.

Kristy led Houdini to the middle of the ring and stopped. She looked up at him, her expression serious, focused. "So, as you're sitting there, are you getting any body memory of your riding experience as a youngster?"

"I am... but it's very different not being able to grab on with my legs."

"You're going to have to rely on balance a lot more than you did before," she said, nodding. "I'm going to walk you and Houdini around the ring a few times so you can get more familiar with how you're going to have to sit a horse now."

"Sounds good." Trevor picked up the reins, placing them correctly in his hands, and readjusted his seat. He'd ridden with an English saddle at his grandparents' farm. This western saddle was like being in a recliner as opposed to a folding chair in comparison. *Nice!*

As Houdini walked, Trevor's body gradually moved more naturally with the horse's movements. He realized right away that the strength of his inner-thigh muscles was sorely lacking for this particular activity. He could work on that at the gym. His stumps weren't long enough for the adductor machine, but he would rig something up with bands.

As he settled into sitting, he realized what leg he had reached about a third of the way to the stirrups. He still had some ability to squeeze. He'd be able to give the horse direction from his legs, by shifting his weight—and through the bit, of course.

"How does it feel up there?"

"Pretty damn good. Better than I'd anticipated. But, despite living at the gym, I'm feeling the total weakness of a certain set of muscles that haven't been tried in decades."

She smiled up at him, dazzling him again. How could he have gotten this far into infatuation in only a few weeks? *Holy crap!*

"Houdini is responding to you being up there as he does the little ones. That says a lot."

"Why do you think," he asked readjusting his grip on the reins.

"Well, I'm guessing, *you* being up there is completely different than when he worked the ranch. You're not spurring the crap out of him. His head isn't forced down with a rope tie-down, and you're not yanking at his mouth."

He looked over at her, and she was studying him.

"You have a real calm and gentle energy up there." Then she laughed. "Not to mention the bromance you two seem to have forged."

He laughed at that, then looked over at her, intentionally smiling. "Well, we're just a couple of old war horses, who have developed an understanding."

Her face softened, and she nodded at that.

Then back to all business, "OK, now I'm going to take off

the lead rope and attach the lunge-line, so you and the big guy can walk the whole ring more on your own."

"OK, I'm ready." Was he really?

She issued a low voiced, *ho*, and Houdini came to a stop. Then after approaching them and giving the horse a pat on the shoulder she released the lead rope and secured the lunge line.

Without waiting for her to get back to the center of the ring, Trevor urged Houdini forward with his voice and a shift in his weight. It worked. Houdini stepped forward into an easy walk.

"So, tell me more about your experience with horses," she said, cocking her head.

"From the time I was in eighth grade, I spent summers and vacations at my grandparents' farm, helping them with the daily stuff, then, at the end of the summer, putting up hay. They had a couple horses I was determined to ride. They weren't very broke at the time, so I spent a lot of time picking myself up off the ground, until we got used to each other and learned a few things. One of them, Lucky, reminds me of this guy," he said, leaning forward to pat his neck. The horse's ears flicked to the side, then back to the front.

"Well, you certainly don't seem to have any fear up there."

"I tend to think of it as a healthy respect." He thought for a minute, then ventured on. "Once you have your legs blown off, there isn't a lot of everyday stuff that's that scary anymore. And like I said, the bottom of my stumps are only about four feet off the ground."

"That's an excellent way to think about it."

The rest of the lesson went great except for a foolhardy squirrel that ran right across Houdini's path, prompting him to stop short. That jostled Trevor, causing him to lose his balance for a moment. He grabbed that horn.

But everything else went smoothly. He and Houdini spent their whole time walking or at a stop doing on-saddle exercises.

When the lesson was over, he asked Kristy to remove the lunge line, so he could walk the horse unassisted over to the dismount platform. When he had him squared at the right spot, Kristy stepped up to hang on to Houdini in case he noticed something interesting and went off to explore before Trevor was finished dismounting.

Dismount and transfer complete, he rolled down the ramp and around, meeting them at the gate of the ring.

Kristy took a step to lead the horse back to the cross-tie area.

"Wait, I'd like to lead him back," he said.

Kristy handed him the reins, and pushing his chair easily with one hand, Houdini allowed himself to be led back to where he would be untacked. The only issue Trevor had was the guy grabbed the hood of his hoodie in his teeth and tried to lead him at the same time.

Once Kristy had the horse clipped into the cross-ties, Trevor leaned forward and pulled his wallet from his back pocket. He extracted six tens, folded the bills and held them up to her.

Even though she was wrangling Houdini's saddle, she took the money from his hand and stuffed it in her pocket. "Thank you," she said, her voice softer than usual.

"Same time next week? I have a feeling I'm going to need to nurse these inner thigh and glute muscles for a few days." He grinned.

Unfortunately, she didn't grin back. Her face remained friendly, but all business. "Yes, same time and day, and yeah, you're probably going to feel this."

He went for the bucket with the brushes.

"Don't worry about that. It's a nice warm day. I'm going to give him a bath."

"Oh, ok."

"See you next week," she said, pretty much dismissing him.

Well crap. He'd had higher hopes for this session. But she *had* softened a little toward him. And, he'd been able to spend precious time with her and that was the main goal anyway.

STANDING IN LINE AT THE FEED STORE TO PAY FOR horse wormer, Kristy watched the strapping young gal further ahead in line, being ogled by the three young cowboys in line behind her. She had jeans and a red hoodie on, that had definitely seen some work at the barn this morning. Her blond hair cascaded down over her shoulders. There was a lovely air of authority about her that bespoke strength and confidence. Kristy realized that was *her* thirty years ago.

The cowboys weren't being at all covert about their appreciation, cocking their heads and checking the back of her out, from head to boot-heel.

Kristy had considered herself fairly attractive as a young woman, but that beauty ship had sailed. She was more concerned about being thought of as interesting looking, at this stage of the game.

Her thoughts went to Trevor, and how well he did during his lesson. Some people are just naturally athletic. And naturally hot. An unbidden flash of Trevor nude, sprawled out on her shower chair under the spray, took a clear and firm presence in her mind.

"Oh, God," she whispered unintentionally. The group in front of her all turned around. She coughed and made like she was looking for something in her purse.

Despite her firm decision to back away from the guy and whatever his intentions were, his image continued to leap into her gray matter without any permission at all.

The young woman finished her business at the counter and turned, giving the guys behind her a look that would peel paint from a post. All three backed up a little. Then she looked at Kristy and smiled warmly, winking as she passed her.

Ah, a nice moment of sisterhood.

After she paid for the three tubes of wormer, she headed back to her truck. Settled in and turning the key, she was hit by the realization that she was really looking forward to Trevor coming back for his next lesson.

"Noooooo!"

CHAPTER 11

"Hey, pass me the sopas, Rob," asked Trevor, fork at the ready to dig into his steaming chili rellenos, his mouth already watering for that first bite.

Rob handed him the basket.

He and the guys had hit Soto's Restaurant after their last workout of the week, heading into a couple of well-earned rest days.

"So, how'd your riding lesson go, Trev?" asked Mike. True interest in his gaze.

"Surprisingly well. But man, it's been three days, and my gluts and adductors are still talking to me," he said shaking his head.

"Have you been able to make any headway with Kristy?" said Mike, shoveling a huge bite of enchilada in his mouth and chewing with gusto.

"Not that I know of." Trevor shook his head and chewed. "She's remaining pretty reserved."

Rob's head popped up from his lunch, giving him a look of haughty satisfaction.

He chose to ignore Rob and focused on his meal. He

knew in his heart that he'd never do anything to hurt Kristy, if only she'd give him a damn chance. Also, his nickel was pretty much up with Rob and all his protective crap. *Enough already.*

Mike pulled out his phone, showing everyone the newest photos of Sophie.

He took the phone from Mike and swiped through all of them. She was so damn cute. The last one of her doing curls with a tiny pink dumbbell.

He turned the phone toward Mike. "Really?"

"She begged for it; besides, it weighs less than her little bear."

He would have liked to have had kids, but Carrie hadn't been able to conceive and after about five years of trying, she'd decided she'd had enough and wanted to move on.

His heart had broken for her. Even now, he clearly remembered all she'd gone through, with what seemed like endless fertility treatments, it still made his heart hurt.

"Dude, hello?" Mike's question interrupted his thinking, and he refocused to see Mike and Rob staring at him.

"Just thinking," he said stabbing at his rice.

"You still doing the show in January?"

"Yep. Really not looking forward to going on prep, though. Every time I do it, it's less fun," he said taking a big cheesy bite of relleno. Realizing his days of cheese-laden anything would be coming to a sad end, and very soon. After this next one, maybe it was time to take a break from it all.

"Yeah, I so get it," said Mike. "I've thought about competing for a year now, but even just the food plan part is going to affect Viv and Sophie, not to mention the early morning cardio, and all the extra time at the gym. Also, with my student teaching starting next semester." Mike lifted his shoulders in question, then dropped them.

"Yeah, being single does have its advantages in the time

suck department." To be honest with himself, being single had lost a great deal of its appeal since he'd met Kristy.

He turned to the younger guy. "You ever thought of doing a show, Rob?"

"Yeah, I've thought about that a lot, after watching you. But I don't know."

Trevor nodded. "Well, if you ever decide you want to, we'll help you out."

Mike nodded, then turned back to him. "So, when is your next riding lesson?"

"Sunday," he said, wondering how he was going to make any headway with Kristy. How was he going to get her to give him a chance? Sure, he'd initially been attracted to her face and body and of course he'd had fantasies about getting laid.

But, in just the few times he'd gotten to spend with her, he'd been taken by what an interesting person she was. His respect for what she did continued to grow. He'd felt a connection from the start. He just knew she'd felt it, too.

Was he totally off with his assumption?

THAT NEXT SUNDAY MORNING, KRISTY FOUND herself experiencing a low level of anxiety, getting ready for her day. The anticipation of Trevor's arrival had gotten her nerves jangling.

She had everything ready ten minutes before his arrival time. Houdini was in the cross-ties. His saddle was propped up against the tack shed wall and his bridle hung from a hook about four feet from the ground, so Trevor could get to it independently.

Why was she so off kilter this morning? She was out of sorts because she'd spent most of the last three days thinking about the guy and how maybe she was being stupid about all this apprehension and avoidance. Hadn't he demonstrated over and over what a good person he was? That he was a worthy man to spend time with? With a group of references standing up for him to boot.

Maybe she was getting close to letting things happen with him? Just the thought of it sent a myriad of conflicting feelings bounding through her—excitement, fear, desire, trepidation.

Trevor's van pulled up to his usual parking spot. Aggie trotted up, and waited for him to unload, and got her expected pets from the guy, before he rolled over to where she and Houdini waited.

God, he looked good. That full-face smile in place. He'd worn a maroon hoodie this time, the color making his blue-green eyes pop. She swallowed, hard.

"Good morning, Trevor."

"Good morning," he said, his smile brightening even more.

"You know the drill, you need to groom your horse before we saddle up."

"Absolutely, I'm on it." He wheeled closer to the bucket holding the brushes and picked out the items he needed, this time grabbing up the hoof pick, too.

She nodded, thinking, good for him, liking his motivation. She groomed the horse's other side.

Grooming went quickly since she'd given Houdini a bath last week, and he still hadn't managed to roll in any manure.

With the horse tacked up, Trevor whizzed over rough terrain, rolled himself up the ramp and his chair was locked and ready for her and Houdini as she walked him into place. She held onto the stirrup on her side, while Trevor climbed aboard, with a bit more agility than the first time. He sat center, adjusting his seat.

Before she could make any move to attach the lunge line, Trevor gathered up the reins, and clucking at Houdini, he pushed forward with his seat and the horse walked forward, Trevor guiding him to the path that ran along the pipe fencing, surrounding the ring.

She followed behind watching the two move nicely along with the horse's gait. Pretty amazed at the independence and appropriateness of his movements along with the horse's. Good body memory there.

Trevor guided him into the center of the ring and stopped, waiting for direction.

"Ok, I'd like you to just do some stretches on the horse before you start. Please do some cross-over stretches, reaching your right hand down to the end of your stumps. Ten on each side."

Trevor sat center, balancing himself with his arms out, then without holding on to the saddle with the other hand, he did ten sets of the stretches reaching way farther on either side of the horse than she thought he could, past the end of his stumps.

When he finished, he turned toward her smiling, again, making her heart race. "What's next?" he asked, sounding like an excited kid.

"How about some twists at the waist with your arms extended out from the shoulder? Same number of sets."

"On it." He completed those, expertly. The guy did intense exercise most days of the week. This was nothing for him.

"So, I'm getting the feeling that you're wanting to dispense with any kind of tether this time, right?"

"Yep."

"You look pretty comfortable up there."

"I am." Trevor readjusted his grip on the reins, ready to go.

"OK, then. Move your horse, on his right lead, so you're walking around the ring along the fence."

Trevor clucked and loosened the reins a bit, scooting

forward slightly with his seat. Houdini walked forward, nicely guided toward the track next to the ring's pipe fencing. He'd made one circle around the ring.

"Can we trot now?"

"Sure, go for it."

Trevor clucked, pushed forward with his seat and squeezed the best he could with his stumps. Houdini moved into a light trot. The look of surprise on Trevor's face was priceless. He managed to sit center on the horse, but he bumped along up there, looking uncomfortable. No longer able to post to the trot, because of having no lower leg, the guy had to sit the trot. Not the easiest or most comfortable part of the riding experience.

"Relax your hips and move your torso back and forth." She hesitated. "Kinda like when you're having sex." As soon as that statement flew out of her mouth, her cheeks heated right up.

He laughed out loud but took the direction. With a little too much gusto at first, then settled into a nice rhythm.

"Your balance is pretty amazing for a guy with no lower legs."

He and Houdini trotted past her. "Well, doing wheelies in a chair, along with all the other stuff you need to learn to do to get around, requires more balance than most people realize. Also, if I were using an English saddle, I would have already bounced right off." He grinned at her and her stomach did a little flip.

"Ok, bring your horse to a walk."

He did, pulling back gently on the reins and sitting still. Houdini settled into a lively walk.

"How would you like to give a lope or slow canter a try?"

"You bet."

"Alright, walk one circle of the ring and when you reach the gate, ask him to canter. And remember, if you find yourself slipping to either side, take your reins in one hand and hold on to that horn."

Trevor nodded and urged the horse forward, sitting nicely as he approached the starting point for the canter. When he approached the gate, he centered himself, squeezed his stumps to Houdini's sides and in an even but directive tone, said, "Canter, Houdini."

To her surprise the horse sprang forward into the faster gait, not quite a canter, but a perfect lope. He didn't need to set any speed records.

Horse and rider were moving nicely together half-way around the ring at that gait, when a dust devil containing a plastic grocery bag swirled into the ring, right in front of them.

She watched in horror as the bag made full contact with the front of Houdini's face causing him to shy, moving abruptly to the left toward the center of the ring, still at a canter. Trevor was jarred off center and sliding slowly to the inside. His outside stump came over the horse, and he hung onto the side of Houdini by the saddle horn like a trick rider.

Trevor let go and landed soundly on his butt. He looked surprised and whipped up but not scared at all. She, however, realized she was terrified. She couldn't stand the thought of anything happening to this man. *Anything!*

Houdini stopped short and shook his head, dislodging the bag from his face, then stepped over to Trevor, stopping and sniffing at Trevor's shoulder. He reached up and rubbed Houdini's cheek, then burst out laughing.

How dare he think this is funny when her heart was doing double time at the thought of what could have happened?

Trevor readjusted his sitting position to where he was facing her. "Kristy, I'm going to get myself over to and up that ramp. Please get Houdini back over there for me?"

He's acting like nothing happened, like he couldn't have been injured by that fall. He'd already commenced to scooting himself over the sand with his very strong arms, toward the ramp, ducking himself under the pipe-fencing when he reached it. When he'd gained the top of the ramp, and pulled himself back up into his chair, she was still standing there.

"What?" he asked.

Houdini walked over, giving her a look like, *Come on, Kristy. Let's get this show on the road.*

"You two," she said with exasperation, walking over and grabbing the horse's reins. Why was she so upset about this? She'd witnessed harmless falls off a horse before, more times than she could remember.

She led Houdini over to the platform. Trevor climbed back on, just like he should after a fall, gathered up the reins and urged Houdini forward to the center of the ring.

Trevor gave her a contemplative look and said, "I think I need to work more on my seat."

"Probably a good idea." *Boy, that guy has the best of attitudes.*

The rest of the lesson consisted of him doing physical exercises, either at a walk or with the horse standing still.

When the lesson ended, her heart rate was back to normal. She took a very large cleansing breath, while she walked Houdini and Trevor over to the ramp, and held the horse while the man transferred back into his chair, still brushing sand from his jeans.

"I'd like for you to please just go relax on the patio."

He rolled down the ramp. "Kristy, I'm fine. I knew it would happen at some point; it's good to have that first fall over with. You wouldn't believe how many times I landed in the dirt, when I was first learning how to do all of this."

"All the same, please just go over there and hang out. I'll join you when I'm done with Houdini."

CHAPTER 12

Trevor sat comfortably on the patio with the mostly silent, ever disinterested Baxter. He brushed off more of the sand that stuck to his jeans. With some real effort, he'd transferred into one of the Adirondack chairs hoping for a nice long conversation, and maybe some more of that lemonade.

He enjoyed watching Kristy brush Houdini down quickly, then lead him to the pasture and turn him loose with the other horses. A smug smile pulled at the side of his mouth.

If he'd known falling on his ass from a horse would have gotten her total attention, he might have done it on purpose during his first lesson. He chuckled low to himself.

Watching her walk over from the barn area and through her backyard up to the patio, it surprised him just how much watching her body in motion warmed him up all over. The crisp, but warm autumn breeze filled his nostrils, as he stretched big in his chair taking an assessment of his physical state. His right butt cheek might give him a bit of trouble, but everything else seemed just fine.

Kristy stepped up on the brick patio and took the Adirondack chair next to his. She turned to him with a little worry on her face. "Are you sure you're okay?"

Taking a chance, he reached for, and with care, lifted her hand from her chair's arm, holding it in his. "I'm fine, really." He cocked his head, pulling up one eyebrow. "If I didn't know better, I'd think you're treating me differently because of my disability."

She looked down at their connected hands. "I don't think so." Sitting back again, her gaze focused on the horses, meandering in the pasture. "It's because I care about you. Probably more than I should." She swallowed hard, then turned a little to face him, and looked up into his eyes. The intensity and earnestness there made him pause.

Holding her gaze, he lifted her hand to his lips for a soft, slow kiss.

A gentle smile slid over her lips. Then gradually, her smile was replaced by a look of hunger, hunger merged with hope. She lifted their hands this time, bringing his knuckles to her lips. The contact of her mouth to his skin brought an unmistakable zap of electricity coursing through his body. *Holy, shit!* That had never happened before.

Kristy let his hand slip from hers, allowing their fingers a lingering brush against each other as the contact eased. His gaze followed her as she walked over to the half-open patio door, then stopped and turned toward him.

His mouth dropped open watching, as she lifted the hem of her henley and with a slow drag pulled it up over her shoulders, leaving her standing there in riding boots, jodhs and a sexy black sports bra.

Dear God. Those curves were just as seductive, just as alluring as he remembered from their make out session in his van. Maybe a little more so.

Kristy turned and disappeared into the house.

Why on earth had he gotten himself into this damn

Adirondak chair? "Fuck," he said to himself under his breath. Adrenaline shot through him. He lifted up on the two arms of the chair and walked himself forward, dropping down in front of the chair onto the bottom of his stumps, then onto his ass. Then scrabbled over to his all-terrain and yanked himself up into it. *Shit, shit, shit this is taking way too long.*

He spun around, pushing forward with big-time effort, making his chair lurch ahead a little off kilter. He adjusted his course narrowly avoiding going up the ramp with one side of his wheels on, one off.

He yanked the sliding glass door open wider. Rolling into her house from the outside brightness he paused to let his vision adjust. All he needed to do was smack headlong into furniture and dislodge himself from his chair wasting more time.

Vision adapted, he sped toward her bedroom. Kristy sat at the end of her bed, leaning back on her arms. Her legs stretched out, crossed in front of her. Boots gone.

"What took you so long?" she asked with a cocky grin.

"Smart ass," he said, rolling over gradually, right to her stretched-out toes.

She sat up.

He wheeled closer and reached for her hand. When his fingers held her firmly, he tugged. She allowed herself to be pulled to her feet and in front of him, her knees almost touching the ends of his stumps.

He pulled her onto him, her legs straddling his lap. Them sitting chest to chest, her beautiful mouth mere inches from his.

There was something in her gaze he'd never seen before, something serene—like the calm that comes when a decision has been made. She closed the space between them and covered his eager mouth with hers. Immediately, deep pleasure from their contact flowed from his mouth outward, throughout his whole body.

Holy, shit! He'd never had a reaction to a kiss like that. He registered her legs closing around him and the back of his chair, bringing her core closer to his burgeoning erection.

What? He was already hard? At this point in his life, he needed to take some pleasurable time to allow things to progress with his body, enough for all systems to be at *go*. Pulling back from the kiss, he whispered against her lips, "You know I'm a lot better at this on a flat surface." And nodded toward her bed.

She grinned and dismounted from his lap, then walked to her side of the bed.

He wheeled right over to the other side and locked up, then practically threw himself from his chair onto the bed, scrabbling toward her.

They met in the middle.

OH, GOD! WAS SHE ACTUALLY DOING THIS?

You bet she was. Totally surprised by the awareness of how sure she felt about this man, this situation, and boy it had been a long time. *In for a penny.*

She rose up on her knees and took his hand in both of hers, guiding it to her breast. The warm contact from his palm even through fabric made her mouth water.

He scooted up closer sitting in front of her, his stumps to either side of her knees. Bringing his other hand up to cover her other breast, and caressing, he said, "Hear tell from women at the gym, that this contraption you're wearing has a reputation of being quite a battle to remove."

Her head had fallen back at his touch, and her breath came

faster. "I ...I ...actually have it down to a science," she said, all breathy.

He dropped his hands from her. "Show me," he said, a grin curling his mouth.

She crossed her arms in front of her, grasping the sides of said garment, and pulled it right up over her head, tossing it to the floor. Where was all of this bravery coming from?

"Beautiful," he murmured. Then, following her action, he quickly removed his hoodie and T-shirt, both in one grab.

She reached up and traced across his large pecs with her fingertips then palms, compelling him to shudder under her hand.

"I want to see you... all of you," she whispered.

Without hesitation, he leaned back and opened his jeans. Then grabbing the waistbands of both his jeans and boxer briefs he pulled them off together, tossing them to the floor.

Dear Lord. He was the most beautiful man she'd ever seen. His skin was smoothed out by all that lovely muscle pushing out through it. His chest hair hadn't grown out all the way from his last show, she thought, as she brushed her palm over the soft pokey fur.

She couldn't wait to get closer to all of that. Not to mention really close to that lovely erection standing there at attention, saluting her.

He interrupted her musings. "So... do you need some help with those riding pants?"

"Oh, no." Thankfully they were stretch. She dropped to her back, flung her legs up in the air and yanked them off her butt and legs, sending them the way of her bra. Then scrambled back to him, laying on her side to match his position, unbelievably not worrying that her stomach was going somewhat the way of gravity.

Slow, but with no hesitation, Trevor lay her back and pulled himself over her. Hip to hip, he rested both elbows on either side of her head, fingertips caressing her temples, his erection pressing nicely against her mound.

His gaze warm, with increasing heat, he kept looking into her eyes as he lowered his mouth to hers. The kiss, light at first, transformed into a deep, drugging spar of lips and tongues. She instinctively widened her knees, and he nestled further in between.

Trevor pulled up from the kiss, and she felt his hips rise. When he settled back down, he entered her body with care. When fully inside, he waited for her to adjust to his presence. His filling her up brought her senses brilliantly alive. Her skin warming all over.

Trevor leaned down, kissing her softly on the mouth. "You, ok?" he asked against her lips.

"Very, ok." His concern made her smile.

Her reverie was interrupted by Trevor pulling almost all the way out then coming back with a very deep thrust, followed by another, and another.

Holy, crap! Sex had never been like this before. The more he moved inside of her the more she felt like she was approaching a six-foot jump. Dangerous, but oh how the danger beckoned. Building, building. A luscious heat coursing, pulsing throughout her entire body. Then, a startling explosion of pleasure, the likes of which she'd never experienced caught her off guard_fanning deliciously out from her core, thrumming all the way to her fingertips and toes.

Holy crap, even her scalp tingled.

Right as she was catching her breath, Trevor's whole body became rigid, and he lifted himself up enough so she could see his face. His features tightened, his eyes closed, and he issued a deep, satisfied groan. When he opened his eyes again his face had morphed into that full-faced smile.

He laughed. "Sweet Jesus! I haven't had sex that great since I was in my forties." He paused, breathless, "Or maybe ever."

He attempted to shift off her, but he wasn't going anywhere.

"Nope. I like you right where you are, mister." She shifted back and forth underneath him, so he would settle back in that perfect spot.

"Yes, ma'am."

Kristy wrapped her arms around his neck and pulled him down into a comforting hug, their heads side by side. He reciprocated by sliding his arms beneath her from either side and enveloped her right back.

Just as they were settled into a wonderful cocoon situation, she had to get up. "Well, shoot!"

He lifted his head. "What?

"I gotta pee."

He chuckled, sliding off her to the side, caressing her shoulder as he went. As she sat up to get up, his hand traveled across her chest, down between her breasts, and over her less-than-flat stomach.

"You are lovely," he, said as though fascinated.

She covered her stomach with her hands.

He leaned in, looking her right in the eye. "All of you."

That sure set her little heart to glowing.

"I'm thirsty," he said, scrambling over to his side of the bed, retrieving his boxer briefs. He pulled those on and transferred.

"I'll get you something to drink."

Settling into his chair, he peered over at her, looking a tiny bit exasperated. "You go pee, woman. I want to explore that wonderfully adapted kitchen of yours." He rolled on, pushing hard, beating her to the doorway.

As he moved on ahead of her, she called out, "There are some sports drinks in the fridge."

"Thanks," he called back.

CHAPTER 13

Trevor cruised through the hall around the corner into the open kitchen. He grabbed the handle of the fridge and yanked with a bit too much force. The door flew open and would have rocked back on its hinges, had he not caught the thing in mid swing. *Whew!*

Rolling in closer, he inspected the interior for something to drink, locating a good old-fashioned root beer. *Yes!* He hadn't had one of those in years. He pulled the bottle out and rolled over, setting it at the kitchen table.

Root beer made him think of his grandparents, which warmed his heart. Then his parents, which did not. They'd totally freaked out when he came back from Vietnam without legs, and with a terrible and scary attitude. Someone they didn't even recognize. He'd been angry with them for a long time about that reception. He'd taken a lot out on them because they were close. And because they loved him, they'd taken it.

"Hey there," Kristy called out stepping into the kitchen in his black T-shirt. He liked that she put on his shirt, and he liked that when he put it back on, it would smell like her. He also liked the lovely, toned legs displayed underneath.

He held up the root beer. "Thanks!"

"Of course, but I thought you'd prefer one of those post sports drinks."

"I get enough of those training." He held up the bottle, smiling. "My grandparents kept these in the fridge all the time."

"You've spoken about your grandparents a few times, but not your parents." She lifted her shoulders in question.

"My folks passed within a few years of each other, back in the eighties. She from cancer and he from a stroke."

"Oh, I'm so sorry."

He shook his head. "We weren't really close," he said taking a swig of his root beer. Did he want to go into this with her? Yeah, why not? "When I came home from Nam, I was very hard to live with. That, and having a legless son, was something they never thought they'd have to deal with. I was their golden boy when I went off to the Marines. But when I came back injured, they never really got over it, never really accepted me back. Made me so angry that even after a decade they never got with the program."

Kristy's face tightened. "I can't imagine not being there for my child after something like that. After war," she said, looking down. "If I'd been able to have a child."

He ached for her, as he had for Carrie. "You're wired differently than most people, Kristy." He wheeled over to her, took her hand, pulling her onto his lap.

She clasped her hands together in front of her chest. "I had really bad endometriosis when I was in my thirties. They do things differently now, but at the time, I was single, and hysterectomy was pretty much the mode."

"I'm so sorry," he murmured hugging her gently.

"Hey, we've had a great time today, and things just got

way too intense. We need to lighten things up here." She jumped from his lap and went over to the counter, to what looked like one of the most ancient boom boxes he'd ever seen and pressed a button. *What, really?* A cassette tape? The Gypsy Kings flew out of the thing, sounding better than he thought it would. "Wow, I haven't heard those guys in a while."

"Thank you for not giving me a hard time about my stone-aged sound system."

He laughed. Who would have thought he'd have better fingers on the pulse of the modern, than his younger girlfriend. *Girlfriend.* Yeah, that's exactly who she was.

She danced around him and the kitchen table, her face alight with joy. Boy did he really like being around her and so looked forward to the time they would spend together. The sex was amazing. Way better than he'd imagined it would be. With a tinge of guilt, he thought of Carrie, and wondered what she would think of all of this.

The guilt eased away, when he imagined that she'd probably kick his ass for waiting so long to jump back into life. She would have hated for him to be lonely or alone, period. He took a deep breath and smiled to himself, finally catching on to that.

The song ended and Kristy came back over and sat on his lap again. She wrapped her arms around his neck and leaned in to kiss him hard and quick on the lips. Her face flushed and eyes bright from dancing around.

"Hey, let me take you out to dinner. I haven't been to Abuelita's in the South Valley in a while. I love their food, and they are way easy for me to get in and out of."

"Yes! I'd love that."

"I'm going on prep soon for my next show. I want to enjoy all the tasty fat I can in the next few weeks."

"Ok, so then next week I want to take you to that new

French place in Albuquerque, so we can get quiche and some decadent pastry."

"It's a deal." He hugged her to his chest, reveling in his new and affirming association with this woman. "But for now I need to get dressed and head out. I need to get a workout in and take care of a few things at home."

She sat back a little from the hug. "Yeah, I've always got stuff around here that needs doing."

"How about I pick you up at six?"

"Perfect."

———

TREVOR COMPLETED HIS LAST, TWO-HUNDRED-pound bench press, then lowered the barbell square to the rack. He sat up and turned toward the guys, stretching his shoulders and neck.

"Kristy and I have a date tonight," he announced, totally buoyant.

Mike rested the dumbbells he'd been working with on the floor and looked over at him. Then leaned in and really looked.

When he sat back up, he had a smug expression on his face. Crossing his arms over his chest, he said, "You got laid."

"Keep your voice down." He leaned over as far as he could without falling off the bench. "Rob is already on my ass about Kristy. I don't need any more crap from him." He sat back up. "But, yeah."

"In the immortal words of *you*," Mike sat back grinning "Don't fuck it up!"

Trevor laughed at that. "I'm going to make sure I don't."

"What's your date plan?"

"Abuelita's."

"Great choice."

"Yeah. It's been too long since I had some of their fantastic rellenos." His mouth watered again thinking ahead about all the cheese he would be missing during prep.

"Kinda feels weird not having Steve here as often."

"It does. Sounds like he's really liking his new job."

"Hey Rob, what's Steve up to these days?"

Rob came over to them and sat down next to Mike. "He's been going to a different gym during the week. It's closer to his work."

"That make sense," said Trevor. "We need to do something after his work hours. Maybe we can go to a Lobo hockey game or something?"

Both Mike and Rob said yeah, at the same time.

"Great!"

———

KRISTY HARDLY EVER WORE DRESSES. COULDN'T even remember the last time she did. But today was different. She felt different. *Oh, God, I have a boyfriend. A relationship. Whatever.*

Every time she thought of what had happened between them this morning, her mouth watered, and she felt like a teenager. That reaction hadn't happened, since, well... since she was a teenager. Being around that guy made her feel like life was still so full of possibility. Although at fifty-eight she was, in many circles, already considered a senior citizen. It was a state of being that she still did not accept.

If she was honest with herself, she couldn't wait for them to get back into her bedroom, or his bedroom or his van for that matter, to repeat this morning's delicious activities. Her mouth watered again. *OMG!*

Standing in front of her mirror, she adjusted the belt of her forest green coat dress, A-line being nicely flattering to her figure.

The nights were getting colder lately, so this dress would be perfect. She wore black tights, and green heeled ankle booties.

Baxter lifted his head and barked twice, interrupting her self-inspection, to announce Trevor's arrival. Aggie trotted over to the door.

She ran her fingers through her hot roller curls and went to the entryway to welcome... her boyfriend? *Yes!*

Trevor had just rolled up to the door when she opened it. A beautiful huge bouquet lay across his stumps. *Oh, man!*

As he came through the threshold, he held it up to her. "You look... great!"

"Thanks," she said, the heat of a blush traveling up her cheeks. What's with all this blushing since she'd met him? She wasn't a blusher.

He wore a navy, long sleeved, semi-formfitting t-shirt, and black slacks. She couldn't wait to run her hands over those amazing pecs, pushing through the t-shirt fabric. *Oh, yeah!*

"Let me get these in water, then I'll be ready. I don't know if I have a vase large enough for these." She took the flowers over and set them on the kitchen table, then rooted around the kitchen. Finally, over the fridge, she located a glass pitcher with a mouth big enough for the bouquet and filled it with water.

She kept stealing quick looks at him while completing her task. Trevor watched her throughout. When she set the pitcher on the table with the flowers in place, she looked over at him. His face was so serene and peaceful, just looking into his face had her taking a slow deep breath and joining him in that peace.

When she stepped up to him, he raised his hand to her, holding it open in invitation. When she joined her hand to his he gave a soft pull, leading her to his lap. Once her butt made contact with his thighs, he wrapped her in a wonderful big hug and held her to him, in silence.

Physical contact with him only served to increase the heated thoughts she'd been having about him all afternoon. He leaned his head to her shoulder, his warm breath fanning her neck.

She sat up quickly. "I want that dinner. Any more of this business and we won't be leaving the house."

He chuckled, as his face lit with one of those wonderful smiles. "Ok, let's get this show on the road."

They headed out, and just as she hit the doorway, she turned to the dogs. "Be the wonderful watchdogs I know you are." Aggie sat there smiling big. Then, if a dog could smirk, that's the expression Baxter flashed her. *That guy.*

The drive to the South Valley from her place went fast. In the evening, they didn't have to deal with passing any tractors. They made it to Abuelita's just as the sun was setting, and great, the parking situation was no problem for Trevor's van. They strolled over to the perfectly assessable entrance. Nice.

The hostess seated them in a center spot of the big room and drink orders were taken.

"So, I was wondering, when the weather gets colder. Does that affect your business?" asked Trevor.

"Some. There are some die-hard riders that keep going all the way through the winter. I'm a licensed occupational therapist. So, when things get too slow, I'll work PRN shifts at the local hospitals doing OT evals for people heading to rehab. Having your own business is a gamble sometimes."

"I'm sure it is. When I was still working, I needed to know I'd get X amount of dollars every two weeks. What you do takes some serious courage."

She laughed. "I really wanted to do horse therapy work. I'd worked for a few other stables, and then when my aunt Milly passed, she left me a nice inheritance. I used a big chunk of it to buy my place."

Trevor grinned. "I have to admit something to you," he said looking down at his menu.

She looked up from hers. "Yeah?"

He cleared his throat and leaned closer to her. "Ever since I used your bathroom that first time I brought Rob to his session, I've had, ah ...fantasies about you and me in that amazing shower of yours." He leaned back with a very unapologetic randy expression on his face.

She couldn't help herself, she burst out with a short laugh and peeked over the top of her menu. "Me, too," she whispered loudly.

"Very good!" His gaze sought hers and his lips opened partially, his tongue running over his bottom lip.

Watching his tongue, her mouth watered. *Oh, my.*

Their waiter stepped up, smiling. "Are you ready to order?"

She refocused on her menu. "I think I'll have the chicken enchiladas, with Christmas."

"I'll have the rellenos with green, extra cheese, and would you bring us two sides of sour cream, too?"

"I'm so jealous. Wish I could eat like that and stay leaner."

"I can't either. This isn't my normal deal. I want to live it up a little before three months of trying to force down endless chicken breasts, ninety-nine percent fat-free ground turkey, and way too many slabs of tilapia with gallons of broccoli." The totally dejected expression that fell over his face as he contemplated his chosen fate almost made her laugh.

"My ex spent a lot of time at the gym. Got fairly fit, too. He talked a lot about competing but never did. While he was with me, anyway." She unrolled her silverware and put her napkin on her lap. Then remembering his judgmental attitude toward her not-as-fit state, she snorted. "I don't really think he had the necessary drive and-or commitment to pull something like that off."

Trevor just nodded, looking at her hard.

"The reason I got weird and walked away from you in the store, was because I was still so angry. Brad met Amber at the gym, you know."

He sat back, clasping his hands in his lap. "I'm so sorry that happened to you. I can't imagine the feeling of betrayal. How long were you two together?"

"Off and on, for about five years. In hindsight it all never really seemed to get off the ground. That's when we decided to try to get serious, when he moved in, when things fell apart." Listening to herself recount their relationship—or lack thereof —really made her liaison with Brad sound terribly lame, and embarrassing.

"When I found them together, I packed his things and put them out in the front yard. It's the only time Baxter showed any real motivation toward anything. I went back out front after an hour or so, and Baxter had gotten into one of his boxes of workout clothes and had torn up three of his favorite gym T-shirts. I laughed so hard. I really needed that."

Trevor was truly focused on her and her words.

"Tell me about your wife." The moment that came out of her mouth, she wished it back.

"Her name was Carrie, and we were married for twenty really great years, before she got sick and passed four years ago."

"I'm so sorry," she said leaning in.

Sitting forward, he gave her a wistful smile. Then it brightened as he searched her face. "You are the one who pulled me out of the staunch widower state that I'd claimed for myself after she died." He took her hand in his. "Thank you for coming down my aisle, at Nature Foods."

She sat back, still holding on to his hand. "Your aisle? The cookie row is definitely mine."

He tipped his head back a little and laughed softly. A laugh as warm as sunshine.

This guy! I want to know him more and more. He kept saying things that pulled her closer to him. Becoming pretty much fearless in the pursuit of a connection. This wasn't at all how she'd operated before, and she loved this newly found power.

The waiter came by with their dinners, placing their plates in front of them with the usual warning not to touch because of their heat. He left and came back quickly, putting two baskets down between them, one of tortillas and one of another weakness of hers—hot sopapillas. *Yes!*

They dug in and the silence that ensued spoke plainly of how hungry they both were.

When they finished their waiter cleared their plates, giving information on the desserts available that evening and Kristy asked that they have more time to think about it.

She rested her crossed forearms on the table. "How's about instead of dessert, we go back to my place and made good use of that shower." Did she really just say that? How brazen could she get? Apparently pretty brazen.

Trevor's eyes went big, and his beautiful face-covering smile came into view. Only this time there was a bit of a predatory gleam to it.

Again, with the mouth watering. *Holy, crap!*

The waiter stepped back up to the table and Trevor said, "Check please," before the guy could get a word out.

CHAPTER 14

Their drive back to her place, quite swift through the Pueblo, had him really hoping that the tribal cops' attention was focused elsewhere.

He turned onto her drive and pulled up to the house. While he dealt with the lift and getting out of the damn van, she jumped out, and let the dogs out.

Despite the uneven terrain, he sped, bumping up to her at the open door, and they both clambered into her house. She slammed the door behind them. When they reached the hall leading to the bathroom, he pulled her onto his lap. Sitting sideways she wrapped her arms around his shoulders, the hug warm and slow. Made him and his urgency ease up a bit.

They stayed motionless, embracing in the hall. He hadn't let himself feel this close to a woman in mind and body for so long. He sensed himself flooded with something over-whelming and amazing. *Love? Already? Nah, can't be.*

Kristy pulled back from their hug and pressed a soft kiss to his mouth. "I know I talked about the shower earlier, but can we just go back in there?" She pointed to her bedroom.

"We can go anywhere you want. That shower isn't going anywhere."

She kissed him again and ran off into the bedroom stripping as she went. The dress went flying, followed by her bra. She kicked off her boots and threw herself on the bed, wrestling with her tights. When they were off, she laid back on the pillows with her hands behind her head. That lovely pose elevated her breasts, just so her nipples pointed up a little. *Beautiful.*

Rolling through the door, up to her side of the bed. "I think you just set a record for speed stripping." He reached out and rested his palm on her hip.

She inched closer to him.

Trevor took his time, caressing up and down the inside of her thigh, then stopping, exploring high in the V of her legs. She was so ready for him.

Kristy's breath hitched from his caresses, then she fixed her gaze on his, "Take off your clothes."

He pulled his fingers away from her moist warmth to lean forward, grabbing and drawing his T-shirt up over his head. He did it slowly, uncovering his skin inch by inch, watching her all the while. When the shirt cleared his head, he dropped it to the floor and looked back over at her studying his chest.

She swallowed hard.

"Scoot over a little."

She did.

He maneuvered his chair close enough to transfer onto the side of the bed and rid himself of his pants and boxer briefs. So glad to see his body was already close to all systems go.

He turned to his belly and crawled up and over her positioning himself, so his lips were right at her belly button. Leaning down he pressed a kiss to her stomach, reaching his tongue down into her navel.

She laughed, "That tickles."

"Well, this will tickle even more," he said, then opened her thighs with his elbows and planted his mouth on her open core, kissing and exploring her with his tongue.

Her soft moans encouraged him further. Her breasts rose and fell as her breath came faster, her head moving back and forth.

Taking his time, he laved and kissed, worshiping her.

She stiffened as she closed in on orgasm.

Breathlessly, "Trevor, I want you up here," she gasped pulling on his shoulders. "I want to finish with you inside."

Pleasuring her like that had made him harder than he could remember. So ready. Pushing himself up on his elbows, he eased himself up with his forearms, so they were face to face. Kissed her a quick hard kiss, then held her and flipped them so she was sitting on top of him and his almost painful erection.

"I want to see you up there," he said. "I want to see you come."

Her eyes grew wide at his words, then her pretty lips pulled into a sensual smile. She drew herself up on her knees, to take him inside. When she sat back down with him buried deep, they both groaned.

Being inside her was unlike anything he'd ever experienced —so amazingly good.

Kristy rose up and down, in a soft careful cadence. Those teasing movements just made him ache for way more intensity from their connection. Grasping her by either side of her hips, he lifted her up, then pulled down hard while pushing up inside her. The sensation was staggering. His breath came fast as though he were running. Kristy supported herself, with her hands on his pecs. Her cheeks, chest and breasts flushed with pleasure. *Beautiful!*

She sat up tall and dropped her head back, her body stiffened, and she cried out softly in completion. She pulsed around him, squeezing, sending him over the edge. He came hard, holding her soft flesh to him as he did.

She collapsed forward, chest meeting chest. Their breathing still coming fast. Holding her close, it hit him. He wanted this woman. Wanted her in his life. Being with her lifted him up from the ordinary to a wonderous place he never wanted to leave.

Their breath returning to normal, they lay in the comfy dim light of a single small lamp across the room, on her dresser. She'd probably planned that. He grinned and chuckled to himself.

"What?" she asked.

"You did that single dim light from across the room thing on purpose, huh?"

She lifted her head, grinning. "Maybe," she said, laughing.

He held her by her shoulders and looked directly into her beautiful blue eyes. "I would find you just as beautiful in the stark light of day, as I do in this dreamy setting."

She pushed her face a little closer to his. "So kind of you to say, He-Man!"

They both laughed at that.

"What about my scars and missing legs? I know that sure detracts from the whole deal."

Kristy eased over on her side, close. "Not at all," she said, running her palm down his thigh cupping the bottom of one stump, then the other. "As corny as it sounds, these are the symbols of your commitment to your family, your friends and your country."

"No one has ever spoken so nicely about my stumps before, thank you."

"Are you staying the night?" she asked.

"Of course," weird that he felt a little insulted, that she'd even asked. Odd, when his before-Carrie history was always to head home after the fun and games were over.

Kristy sat up and scrambled to the end of the bed. "I need to check on the horses and close up for the night. You just relax."

He sat right up. "No way." He clamored to the side of the bed, gathering his clothes. "I'm coming too."

After getting dressed, they headed out to the barn. Kristy made sure everyone was all secure in their stalls, except for Houdini. He hung out over in the small training ring, nickering to get their attention. Kristy had handed Trevor a carrot to give Houdini.

He headed over to the guy, Aggie walking along with him. When he reached the pipe fencing, Houdini poked his head between the bars, nosing around. Probably smelling the carrot in his lap. He lifted the treat up to the horse's mouth, letting him take a solid bite out of it. The sound of his crunching and the smell of carrot and horse were both strong pulls to memories of long ago. Bosque Farms was a peaceful place. The peace and quiet such a balm, compared to the noise and bustle of Albuquerque. Kristy had picked a perfect place for her business and a perfect place to live.

"You two done over there?"

"Almost," he called back. He gave Houdini the rest of the carrot, then wheeled over to the gate to double check the lock. The horse followed along with him and stuck his head between the bars again. He paused scratching the guy's forehead. "Good night, Houdini."

Rolling over to where Kristy waited for him, he took her hand and kissed the back of her fingers. "This is the best date I've ever been on."

She laughed and squeezed his hand back. "Me, too."

"I'M SO THRILLED YOU COULD JOIN US FOR BONNY'S soccer game this morning," said Lucy leaning her forearms on her knees.

"It's so good to see you, Kristy," Viv chimed in. Then her expression turned mischievous. "I hear you've been seeing more of Trevor."

All of him. "Yeah," she said, issuing a little sigh she had not intended.

Both Viv and Lucy stared at her, like, yeah... and?

"OK, yeah I've seen a *whole* lot of him," she said to them grinning.

Both cheered and grabbed an arm from either side.

"Details," coaxed Viv. "I don't mean blow by blow," she said winking.

Kristy touched the side of her mouth with a fingertip. "Well, we haven't gotten to that but give me some time."

That prompted major hooting and side hugs.

Abruptly, Lucy stood. "Bonny has the ball!"

She and Viv joined her standing and yelling big time support for Bonny, as she made her way up the field. What a cutie, that Bonny, and smaller than the other girls on her team, but she was a scrapper. Just like her mom and auntie.

She realized in the past with Brad, she was never all that self-disclosing about their life together. She laughed under her breath. Maybe that was because she really didn't have much to disclose with him, and at that moment she also realized just how subtly and not so subtly judgmental he'd been to her, all along. Under the guise of being helpful. *Ugh!*

Bonny darted and dodged her opponents as she moved the ball closer to the goal, stopping ten feet in front of the goalie. Then with a swift kick from her left leg, the ball shot forward at an odd angle, faking the goalie out, going straight into the net.

Bonny and her teammates jumped up and down, yelling

and screaming. She looked over to them in the bleachers with a big grin, giving them a thumbs up.

Lucy gave her one right back and with eyes all bright with unshed tears, she said, "I love this point in time with my girl. We're still pals. A couple more years and I'll be enemy number one."

Vivian put her arm around her sister. "You don't know that."

"Right?" said Kristy in support. "You could continue on just as you are."

Lucy smiled a wistful smile. "Yeah, it would be great if she and I could skip those rough years, but… we'll make it through either way."

The game ended soon after Bonny's goal and the three of them climbed down from the bleachers and ran out to congratulate the amazing Bonny. Enfolded in a hug times three, Bonny laughed, chanting, "Blitz is number one, Blitz is number one."

When the hubbub settled down, Kristy, Viv, Lucy and Bonny headed toward the parking lot.

When they reached their respective cars, Lucy called out to her. "Hey Kristy, would you like to join us for lunch? We're having carne adovada tacos. Rudy has had the stuff in the crock pot since like, six this morning."

Really tempting. She hadn't been over to Lucy's since she'd hosted a party for their Mostly OT women's group back in August, but she had to work in a couple of hours and had some things to prep for. "I'd love that, but I have someone coming for a ride soon. Please don't stop asking, though."

"No worries," Lucy said, stepping forward for a hug. After releasing her friend, she turned to Bonny. "Congrats on your goal and win, today!"

"Thanks, Kristy!" Bonny came forward for a hug, too.

"Have a great rest of the weekend you guys," she called as

she headed away to her truck. The three of them waved with enthusiasm.

She drove out of the parking lot, noticing that her spirits had been markedly higher, more buoyant over the last few weeks than they had been in a very long time.

She replayed the image of Trevor above her, looking into her eyes, pushing into her body. Her mouth watered. *Holy crap!* If she didn't get this fantasy under control, she'd need to pull over. That whole business made her laugh out loud.

Swallowing hard, she pulled back from the fantasy, just holding onto the way he looked naked in her bed. "Oh, boy. Can't wait to get that guy out of his clothes again."

When did she get so bold? This was new for her. Maybe she felt freer about this relationship, because... maybe it was right? Good for her? She sure hoped so. Hope. Her new watchword, she thought, grinning.

Her drive home was quick, as the soccer field was only a couple of miles from her place. She opened the gate and drove through, pulling up to the house.

Baxter was in his usual spot and Aggie came trotting up to her for some pets. After petting Aggie, she called out, "Hey Baxter!" He chuffed a couple times.

Walking into and through her house, then into the kitchen, she noticed the light blinking on her answering machine. The readout announced one message. She set her purse down and pushed the button to start the message. "This is Updated Imaging, reminding you of your appointment." It droned on about time, date, please check in fifteen minutes early. *Blah, blah, blah.*

Good thing for the reminder, she'd forgotten all about the appointment—with her mind crammed full of so many nicer thoughts lately.

She checked her wall calendar to make sure she hadn't

double booked any riders for that date and time since she'd have to go up to the city for the mammogram.

Nope, all clear, good.

SITTING ON A WORKOUT BENCH, TREVOR disengaged the exercise band he had around his right stump, mid-thigh, attached to one of the sides of the Smith rack that Steve was using. He'd done the left side first. He just might want to continue riding horses and was determined to increase the strength of his inner thighs.

All during the activity, with every rep he completed, his thinking kept being drawn back to the cadence of his thrusts while making love to Kristy.

Good, God. He couldn't remember sex being that good, ever. That thought sparked a bothersome twist of guilt, when thinking of Carrie. Their sex was great, but their last times she'd been sick and that had changed everything.

Sighing, he knew Carrie would approve of him finding connection with another woman, after four years of being a widower. She'd encouraged it, right close to the end. She'd told him as they sat at home, her on hospice, them watching TV together. She'd turned to him, muted the TV, and looked him right in the eye, and told him she'd come back and pester him in ghostly form, if he stayed alone too long.

He chuckled to himself at the memory of that conversation, even though heartbreakingly bittersweet.

Clearing his throat, he rolled over the front desk and returned the exercise bands he'd checked out. On the way back to the guys, an extremely fit and attractive young woman stepped right in front of his chair, halting his progress. He'd seen her working out from time to time.

He stopped, sat back, and draped one shoulder over the

back of his chair, giving the woman his best, *yeah, and what?* look he could muster.

"Didn't you do the summer show at the Kiva?"

"I did."

She took a step closer. "Are you doing the one in January?"

"I am," he said nodding.

"So am I," she said striking a bit of a pose that showed off her excellent figure. "Maybe we could train together."

"I don't think my girlfriend would appreciate that."

Her expression darkened, and she dropped her arms at her sides. "She wouldn't have to know."

He leaned a bit forward. "But I'd know. Besides, I've already got training buddies." The poor thing shriveled a little before him, and he felt bad for her. "Are you working out with anyone?"

"Not really. My sister comes with me once in a while. This is my first show, and I'm pretty much on my own," she said rubbing her hands up and down her arms. "I've done a lot of reading about how to do all the things. And I've been working with a posing coach, whose card I found on the bulletin board up there.' She pointed toward the front desk.

"How old are you?" he asked.

She stood tall again, "Thirty-two," she said.

"Well, I'm sixty-nine."

Her eyes widened in apparent surprise. "Wow! I thought..."

He laughed good-heartedly and leaned forward, "Trevor Drury," he said, offering his hand.

"Raquel Torres," she leaned forward shaking his hand with some strength.

"If you're serious about having people to train with, I can talk to the guys." He pointed over to the area where they were all congregated.

"I've seen you all over there. You all look tight. Isn't there a woman with you guys sometimes?"

"Yeah, she joins us when her schedule permits. It's a good group. What were you going to do next?"

"The leg press."

"Well, why don't you go do that, and I'll check in with them and let you know."

"Ok, thanks," she said looking down, posture totally lax. All bravado gone, she stepped away toward the leg press machines.

Trevor pushed toward where the guys were. When he pulled up to them, Mike gave him a minorly judgmental, majorly quizzical look.

Trevor cocked his head toward the guy, "Really?"

Mike held up his hands and shrugged his considerable shoulders.

"Her name is Raquel and she's training for her first show... alone."

Mike and Rob said, "Oh," in unison. Steve was too busy watching Raquel work out on the leg press.

"I wanted to check with you guys to see if she could train with us. I find myself feeling... I don't know, kind of... protective. Getting ready to compete is a long, hard road, and there is a lot to learn, especially for the first time."

He waited for a moment.

"Yeah, sure," said Mike, still looking a bit unconvinced.

Rob stood up, smiling, "Ok!"

Trevor turned toward where Steve was standing. He stood at the frame of the Smith rack they'd been working with, his hand caressing slowly up and down the frame as he watched Raquel work out.

"Steve?" Nothing. Trevor waited, guessing by his actions, he'd be A-OK with the plan. "Steve!"

"What?" He turned around to the group, looking unfocused with a big grin on his face.

"Are you OK with Raquel training with us?"

Realizing he'd been caught in his admiration, Steve's face flushed red. He cleared his throat. "Yeah, sure," he said, trying to sound like he didn't care.

He, Mike, and Rob all broke out laughing.

"She's too old for you, Steve. She told me she's thirty-two."

"Four years is nothing, compared to your and Kristy's age-gap. Cradle-robber!"

The guys all laughed again. He couldn't believe he was miffed for a nano-second, then dropped his head back a bit and joined right in.

CHAPTER 15

Kristy always paired doctor appointments when having to drive up to Albuquerque—like today's mammogram—with something fun. This time was lunch with Viv and Lucy at Stanley's Tavern near the mall. With her annoying appointment over, she set her sights on the Tavern. It was a fun place with a nice mix of New Mexican dishes along with a lot of standard American favorites.

As over-the-top as it was, fat-and carb-wise, she'd had her heart set on a Monte Cristo sandwich with fries. Just thinking of it made her mouth water.

And lately, anything mouthwatering drew her thoughts to Trevor. *Geez! That guy!*

She was following Trevor's path eating heartily right now, then planned to focus on her own reduction plan when he went on prep for his bodybuilding competition. That would make it easier for them to eat together with him not feeling as bad about his spare and repetitious meals. Hey, maybe she'd start going to the gym, too. Weight-bearing exercise was certainly timely at this point in her life. Not that riding and horse chores didn't do a lot for her already, but she could always add a bit more activity, focusing on different parts.

She opened the door to the eatery, spying Lucy and Viv waving from the back. Kristy smiled and returned the wave. Threading herself through the tables and chairs to get to her friends, she thought about how lucky she was to have these two women in her life.

After Brad left her, she'd pulled into herself and cut off a lot of her socializing. She realized now how dumb that was, because staying away from the people she valued when struggling with something only made her feel worse.

"How are you gals?" she asked taking her seat and dropping her big red purse to the right of her.

In unison they said, "Good, how about you?" Then laughed.

"I'm great!"

With seriousness, Lucy asked, "How's things with Trevor?" Real caring coming through her words, not feeling nosey or prying at all.

"He's pretty great, too." She leaned forward and clasped her hands together around her plate. "You know it's been so... so great to take that step, to trust again. Because opening to the possibilities with him is making me feel like, like ...a lot of other things are possible too."

Lucy sat back and smiled at her. "I'm so happy for you. He's completely avoided entanglements since his wife died. It's high time he got back in the game. Same with you, my friend."

Kristy grinned back. "How's Bonny and soccer going? That was fun, the other day. I hadn't been out to anything like that in a long time."

"The season is almost over. They play their final game next Saturday. The Bosque Blitz are in the running for league champs."

"I'd love to go!" She was really looking forward to this.

"Great! We'll all go, we'll bring the guys, and then we'll go over to our place for, hopefully, a victory party," said Lucy.

"That sounds really fun," said Viv. "You'll get to meet my baby girl, Sophie," Viv said with love just gushing out of her. "But Grandpa Trevor will probably hog her the whole time."

Grandpa Trevor, huh? "Can't wait to meet her and see Trevor get all gooey with a baby."

"Once he gets her on his lap, it's over. No one else even tries to get a turn holding her anymore when he's around," Lucy chimed in, grinning.

"How'd the big squeeze go?" asked Viv, unrolling her silverware from the cotton napkin.

"About as well as to be expected."

"Well, it's over for another year," Lucy observed.

"Yes!"

The waitress stepped up. "Are you all ready to order?"

"I am," Kristy said, "I looked up the menu online. I'll take a Monte Cristo sandwich with fries and a lemonade."

"Wow, a total Carb-ageddon. I'm in!" Viv said laughing. "I'll have the same."

Lucy stuck with her standard. Green chili cheeseburger with seasoned fries.

"You're missing out, sis'," said Viv shaking her head.

———

"ALL HAIL THE BOSQUE BLITZ CHAMP!!!" yelled Mike as the whole family and entourage made their way from the cars to Lucy and Rudy's house. Her dad giving Bonny a piggyback ride all the way. Vivian and Mike strolling up the walk, with Sophie on her hip. Kristy was so happy to be immersed in all the laughter, excitement, and camaraderie of this amazing group of people. She and Trevor cruised together at the back of the crowd.

Kristy assisted Trevor, pulling him backward up over the one step onto their porch, then he rolled solo into the house. As they entered, Kristy was impressed by how Lucy and Rudy had set the house up so perfectly for the party that morning. The aroma of queso in the crockpot made her mouth water. Soccer-themed decorations highlighted the den and dining room where the table was already set with plates, silverware, and napkins, also soccer-themed.

Bonny was a lucky kid to have parents that loved her so and supported her so much. Her own parents loved her, she knew. But they had been so consumed by their own pursuits that they never made it to even one of her horse shows. Her aunt had been the one who took on that role. *God, love her.* She really missed her Auntie Milly.

"How about we go settle in the den?" suggested Trevor. She could see there was a definite spot arranged for his wheels in the constellation of chairs set up in there.

"Sure, sounds good."

Rudy, the chef of the house, bustled around the kitchen. "I'll just get these pans into the oven for a warm-up," he said smiling at the group. "Shouldn't take more than twenty minutes or so." Heads nodded all around as various members of the group settled into chairs in the den.

Viv came over with Sophie in her arms. "Wanna visit with Grandpa, Sophie?" The little girl already had her arms straining toward Trevor.

"Gampa!" said Sophie, trying to wiggle out of her mom's grasp to get to him. Viv laughed as she attempted to make a safe transfer of her girl.

Right as Sophie landed on Trevor's stumps, she crawled up his chest and grabbed him around the neck, burying her head under his chin. The full-face smile of love and pride on Trevor's face yanked at her heart like crazy. She realized she was smiling big too, and that she had been doing a lot more of that in the last several weeks.

Her phone pinged and she pulled it from her back pocket. Weird, one of those messages that must have been jumping around cyber space for a couple of days. Didn't help that she'd hadn't paid a whole lot of attention to her cell over the last two days, either. A call from her doctor, specifically her doctor's cell.

She put her hand to Trevor's arm and leaned closer to his ear. "I'm sorry, I need to take this."

He leaned over and gave her a soft kiss on the cheek. "I'll be here," he said, then returned his attention to Sophie.

Kristy walked down the hall and to the right. When she closed the door of the bathroom, she dropped the toilet seat and sat. Staring at her phone she hesitated then tapped the button for the waiting voicemail. "Hello Kristy, it's Dr. Rodriguez, I'm sorry to have to tell you, your mammogram showed some anomalies. I don't normally do this over the phone, but could you come in first thing on Monday so we can talk about it? Just come at eight and I'll see you first."

Kristy sat staring into the tub across from her. That yearly quiet worry now held reality. She felt her face heat up, while dark tendrils of fear spiraled through her. Her mouth watered and she swallowed hard. Her imagination was too great for her own good. She saw herself bald and nauseated as she'd seen friends experience in the past. Some of them had made it through, some had not.

The urge to burst out crying came sharp and with ferocity, but she breathed through it. That would have to wait until she was alone. She stood up from the toilet pivoting to look in the mirror. She looked like she'd seen a ghost, and she had. Her buddy LeeAnn was two years gone now. *Oh, God!*

Footsteps came up to the bathroom door. "Hey, Kristy,

we're going to sit out on the patio since it's such a nice warm day."

She was too busy thinking of LeeAnn and didn't answer.

"Kristy?"

Still couldn't bring herself to respond, as she tried to keep her breathing normal.

"Kristy, I'm coming in." Lucy opened the door and looked at her. She knew Lucy was greeted with the sight of a hot, red face and wide eyes.

"Sweetie, what is it?" she asked turning on the bathroom fan.

Standing, she felt her eyes grow bigger. "My mammo ...it's ...it's wrong."

"Oh, Kristy," said Lucy, taking her gently into her arms. Which was probably what kept her on her feet at that point. She held onto Lucy, the wonderful lifeline, knowing she might be depending on her and the rest of the Mostly OTs a lot, in the coming days.

Lucy helped her back to the toilet seat and sat across from her on the side of the tub. "Ok, what did your doctor say?"

"She said there were anomalies. Wants to see me on Monday."

"Anomalies could be a lot of different things, and not necessarily terrible. You've got to stay in the here-and-now, or you're going to drive yourself crazy waiting for Monday."

Lucy took both of her hands. "I get it if you want to go home, but I think it would be better for you not to be alone just now. What do you want to do?"

She took a long slow breath, feeling some of the heat leave her face. Took another one. "I want to stay, and I think I need to eat something. Food is always a calmer-downer for me."

"Great. We have plenty waiting for you out there." Lucy took her hands, squeezing her fingers. "I am here for you in whatever capacity you need me, Kristy. Ongoing, OK?'

She nodded at her wonderful friend. "I know you are. Thank you, Lucy," she said, squeezing Lucy's fingers back.

A staccato knock came through the door. "Hey you guys. What's going on?" Viv's firm inquiry demanded an answer.

Lucy leaned in, "Do you want me to beg off for you?"

"No, I might end up needing the strongest team I can muster."

Lucy opened the door for Viv, and the beautiful Amazon pushed her way in. "What's up?"

Kristy just couldn't verbalize it again, and she nodded to Lucy and looked down at the blue fuzzy rug on the floor.

"Abnormal mammo."

"Oh, shit," said Vivian, and her new friend grabbed her up in a big fortifying hug, practically lifting her off the floor.

"We're focusing on the fact that it could mean a lot of different things, not all horrible. And Kristy is staying for food. We are going to present ourselves as though we just had girl talk in the ladies' room and go about our business when we return to the guys."

"Yes, exactly!" Kristy initiated a long slow breath, Lucy and Viv joining right in. They all held it for a few seconds and released.

Kristy's thinking and feelings were still a whirlwind of emotion, but how wonderful of these women, lending her their strength. Her face no longer felt as hot. "Is my face still purple?"

"No," said Lucy, "Just a little pink."

Vivian went over to the sink and grabbed the blue washcloth, wetting it with cold water. She wrang it out, and folded it into a perfect rectangle, then held it out to Kristy, kindness emanating from her face.

"Thank you," she said, taking the cloth and pressing it to her cheeks. The cool moist compress helped to distract her from the unpleasant possibilities.

She rinsed out the cloth and hung it over the side of the sink. "Ok, let's go."

When she opened the door, Rudy and Mike were leaning against the wall across from the bathroom. Trevor was parked to Rudy's left. Bonny peaked around the door jamb only far enough for Kristy to see one wide blue eyeball.

"Oh, my God!" Kristy was on them like a chicken on a Junebug. "Were you all eavesdropping?"

"I just got here," said Trevor, raising his palms in supplication.

Rudy stayed quiet and shook his head, no.

Mike, to Rudy's right, held Sophie under his arm like a football, and raising the other as though trying to make a point, his face in total apology mode, dropped his head a little. "Well, since you had the fan on all we could hear was a bunch of voices."

Bonny's eyeball slipped quickly out of sight.

Kristy stepped out of the bathroom, stopping in front of the men, looming over them—as much as a five-foot-four woman can loom over three tall men. She focused more on Trevor, so she could actually loom, since he was in a chair. "I don't believe you guys!" She jammed her fists on her hips. "I thought you knew women-in-the-bathroom-time is frickin' sacred, damn it."

All three of them kept their mouths shut, watching her for what—direction?

She let her arms fall to her sides. "OK, let's eat."

CHAPTER 16

After the party, she and Trevor headed back to her house. Kristy sat back in the passenger seat of his van, looking like she totally belonged there. Her arm extended between them, as she rested her hand on his shoulder. Occasionally she would squeeze lightly and brush her hand back and forth.

Grinning to himself, he realized he must be really horny, because just the sensation of her hand moving on his shoulder prompted his needing her, bad.

Keeping his eyes on the road, he said, "You know what's going to happen the moment we close the door to your house, right?"

"Tell me?" she asked grinning.

"Well, I'm going to throw myself onto your nice big couch and drag you on there with me."

"Is that so?" she asked, giving his bicep a nice squeeze.

"It is so," he said, with maybe a little more confidence than he felt. She could make this way more complicated if she decided to be a smart-ass and run from him.

"We will see," she said, her expression turning haughty.

He pulled the van into her driveway, then eased it up to the front door of her home.

She jumped right out, pet the dogs, and ran into the house closing the door after her.

Great. She was going to pay for this. A plan of action formulated in his mind as he worked the lift to vacate his van. Finally on the ground, he closed up his vehicle and Aggie came over for a pet. He obliged.

He rolled over to the door. She'd better not have locked that damn thing. But the knob turned easily. Entering the house, he closed the door and locked it. She wasn't on the couch as he'd hoped she'd be. *Shit.*

He rolled further into the house, and catching the sound of the shower running, his eyes widened. Speeding down the hall, around a sharp corner and into her bathroom, he was greeted by the sight of naked Kristy standing under the spray, head back, smoothing her drenched hair back. Water sluiced down over the curves of her body. The obscured image from the glass, and the steam billowing around her, made her appear to be some sort of otherworldly creature.

He was instantly hard. *Holy Christ!* Tearing at his clothes he couldn't get them off fast enough. He practically threw himself from his chair to the floor and wrestled with his pants. When he was finally naked, he scooted over and around the glass wall to get to her. She took his hand and held on as he scrabbled up onto the heavy teak shower chair.

Taking her hand, he pulled her onto his lap, loving her wet skin slip-sliding against his. Kristy wrapped her arms around his neck and initiated a kiss that set him on fire. Her tongue entered his mouth without hesitation and explored him, as he caressed her water-slippery breasts.

She pulled back from the kiss and slowly slid down from his lap to her knees in front of him. With a playful grin, she reached up and put her hands to his pecs, caressing down his chest, over his abs and finally letting her palms rest on his stumps. Then moving in, she took his erection in both hands, her warm, wet mouth covering him.

Sweet Jesus!

Later, spooned in her bed, his amazing chest to her back, they both snuggled deep into her soft covers. His hand covered her breast as he settled into sleep. That hand protecting the breast with the anomaly.

She really needed to tell him. But when? Things were so wonderful right now. The super hopeful part of her wanted to just enjoy this amazing time, with this amazing man. Let it go where it would.

But responsible Kristy's sense of right and wrong pounded through her brain, *tell him, tell him,* a headache threatening. She would, and soon, but not tonight.

KRISTY AND TREVOR STROLLED FREELY THROUGH Albuquerque's botanical gardens. The days of having to fight the big crowds had passed. The sky was gently overcast, with a comfortable temperature. They practically had the place to themselves in late October. Only the work crews and an occasional, green-thumbed person strolled by now and then. They stopped in one of the lovely alcoves. Trevor pulled her onto his lap and wrapped his arms around her. She leaned her head on his shoulder. The air was crisp, smelling of harvested vegetation. All should be well and still in her soul, in such a peaceful place, entwined in the arms of this man she loved.

But it wasn't. Not by a long shot. The notion of keeping a secret from him felt just awful, a weight that she needed to release. He deserved better than this from her.

Kristy sat up on his lap, "Trevor, I have to tell you something."

He took her hand in his, kissing her palm. "OK, what do you have to tell me?"

She swallowed hard. "I had a suspicious mammogram," she blurted out, exhaling a pent-up breath she didn't realize she'd been holding.

His body stiffened ever so slightly in response, maybe just reacting to the sudden cool breeze that had swept over them at the time of her announcement, hopefully? His gaze remained focused on her, but his eyes widened just a hair, and was that a twitch of his jaw just then?

He tightened his arm around her a little. "So, what's the plan?" he asked softly.

"Well, next Thursday I have to go in for a surgical biopsy, and then we see what we see."

He nodded, looking down at her hand in his. His Adam's apple bobbed with a swallow.

She leaned back a bit, "Are you OK?"

"Sure, sure," he murmured. Then he pulled her closer to him.

For some reason not being able to see his face gave her pause. They sat together in a weird silence. As they lingered the wind presented itself in earnest, whipping leaves and dirt up around them.

She pulled back, looking at her watch, eleven o'clock. "What do you say we head over to the Frontier for an early lunch?"

"Great idea!" he responded with a hair too much enthusiasm. Something was definitely off.

When they parked on Yale Avenue, she asked "Are you sure Frontier is Ok, being on prep and all?"

He engaged the motor for the back door of his van, then the lift. "Oh yeah this is my cheat meal for the week." His expression and state seemed pretty darn normal as the lift lowered.

Hmmm. Maybe she was just imagining things. Her thinking did tend to run a bit wild when fear and doubt came to call. They strolled toward the entrance, at a comfortable pace.

When they entered the place and got in line to order, she looked up at the huge menu board trying to choose. She decided to treat herself to some chili-cheese fries.

Trevor ordered a green chili cheeseburger and fries, along with a Frontier cinnamon roll.

"You gonna let me get in on some of that action?" she asked, right after the words 'Frontier roll' came out of his mouth.

He laughed. "Of course, woman. My roll is your roll."

Oh, thank God. He's my good old Trevor. She squeezed his hand.

They had just settled into a window table, when their big red order number flashed on the sign ten feet above them.

"I'll go," Kristy said with a cheerful smile, hopping up from their table.

Trevor nodded, and he watched her jog off. He needed a moment alone to compose himself after the bomb she'd dropped on him at the gardens.

Holy Christ! He rubbed his cheeks with his palms. She had no idea what she might be facing. His heart bled for her at the thought of all the miserable experiences associated with cancer treatment. Ones he'd watched Carrie face. He had to get himself in a space where he could deal with this. He did five box breaths, but it didn't do much, still finding himself sitting ramrod straight.

Jesus! He hadn't felt this kind of anxiety in years. His

mouth watered. He could feel sweat forming down the middle of his back. His heart pounded.

Ok, he needed to stop this. He was overreacting. But was he? He swallowed again. Taking another long slow breath in and out, just as Kristy came back to the table with a tray laden with food he no longer had any taste for.

"Here you go," she said with a big smile, placing his burger and fries down in front of him. She put her plate at her spot, and the Frontier roll in the middle of the table between their plates.

He plastered a smile on his face and grabbed his burger taking a healthy bite. As long as he kept eating, he wouldn't have to talk. Because he didn't know what the hell he was going to say to her. The whole deal was grim and possibly worse than grim.

He watched her dig into her chili-cheese fries. Eyes closed, her enjoyment was written all over her sweet face. He loved seeing her like this, healthy, happy, playful. Terror bounced through him, at the mere notion that cancer might rob her of all those wonderful things.

Her eyes opened and fixated on him, and her expression pulled into one of concern. "Are you Ok? Your face is red." She wiped her fingers on her napkin and put her hand on his wrist.

"I'm guessing it's physical changes from being on prep, no worries," he lied, and took another bite of his burger.

They finished their meals, his conversation spotty and somewhat forced. He kept trying to think of things to talk about, but his brain was engaged in all the horror that might be awaiting her. And *Christ on a crutch* every time he looked her, he couldn't help imagining her wan and frail, with a scarf arranged on her head to cover her baldness.

Swallowing hard, he took the last bite of his lunch that he could stand and pushed the plate away.

"Wow, that's not like you, to not gobble up everything on a cheat day." She cocked her head and pulled her eyebrows up in surprise.

"Something's off with my guts," he lied. "I think I really need to head out."

"Want me to come home with you? Help you get comfy?"

"Na, I'll be fine." He couldn't look her in the eye. *Jesus Christ, I can't believe this. How can I be facing this twice in one lifetime?*

He pulled back from the table, Frontier roll forgotten. Kristy gathered up her purse. Her hand came to rest on his shoulder as they left the restaurant, the soft presence there bore down on him like a hundred-pound weight.

When they reached their vehicles, she stood by while he got in with the lift. After he'd engaged the tie-downs, closed the back doors, and started up the van, he rolled down the passenger window.

They had met at the Frontier earlier to begin their excursion. "Go ahead, I'll wait until you walk down to your truck, and you're situated before I take off."

Confusion tightened her face. "Ok," she said softly almost as if she were talking to herself. She looked up into his face, with nothing but confusion on hers.

"I'll talk to you soon," he said.

CHAPTER 17

Unfocused, Kristy lunged Houdini, prepping him for the next session. She'd forgotten to tie back her hair, and the wind whipped it about her face, spurring her irritation up a notch.

It had been three whole days and an embarrassing too many attempts to contact Trevor, with no response. She knew her abnormal results might upset him, but she never thought he'd ghost her like this. Her emotions had pretty much built up into quite a dust devil. And were threatening all-out-storm level.

Houdini must have been feeling something off because she wasn't focused on her work like she usually was. He stopped trotting in the circle around her and turned in facing her, then backed up a little, tugging Kristy into the total here and now.

She loosened the lunge line to stop the horse from pulling and walked toward him. When she reached him, she rubbed his cheek. "I'm sorry, dude. I'm having a tough time." And just like that, tears erupted and fell. She leaned her forehead into his neck, finally letting loose to all her sadness, fear, and disappointment, and let herself go with a good cry.

He stood with her, occasionally lowering his head, rubbing the side of his cheek against Kristy's thigh.

After she didn't know how long, she stilled and drew a deep cleansing breath. She felt a little better, the tension over it all gone, for now. Leaning in, she wrapped her arms around Houdini's neck breathing in his wonderful horsey scent and gave his thick neck an easy hug. "Thank you."

He breathed in deep and issued a sigh-snort.

"Ok, back to work." She stepped back into the center of the little training ring, and clucked Houdini into motion to finish his warm-up, her own vigor renewed. Megan would be there soon, and they'd both be ready for her.

The familiar SUV pulled into her parking area under the cottonwoods. Megan's door flew open and with great effort she ran over to the cross-tie area where Kristy had just finished tacking Houdini up.

"Hello, Megan!"

The girl stepped up to her, with a smile so excited and bright it yanked at her heart. "Hi, Kristy!"

Then she sidestepped over to Houdini, who already had his head lowered and was sniffing at the girl's knee.

"What's new with you, Megan?"

"Well, it's always so great to be here." Then her expression got serious, and she dropped her arms. "But you know, sometimes I get really tired of the kids at school staring at me as I walk down the hall." Her face scrunched up with frustration.

Kristy motioned Megan to sit with her on a couple of the white plastic lawn chairs lined up against the tack shed. When settled in, Kristy turned to her. "I'll bet you're tired of it."

"When I was really little, I couldn't walk at all." She crossed her arms over her chest. "It took me a long time to walk on my own. I'm proud of my walk, damn it!"

Kristy smiled. She'd never heard the girl swear. "I'm proud of your walk, too."

She sat back against the wall. "I know you've probably heard this many times, but most people aren't jerks. Staring is one of the things humans do when they have no real experience or knowledge of something. They're curious."

"Sometimes, Carmen in my math class makes fun of me by copying my walk."

"That's pretty jerky. But still, she's one of those who feels uncomfortable with something she doesn't understand. I'm sorry Carmen is a brat-face."

That made Megan laugh. "You know, if I was still using a cane, I'd feel like whacking her with it," she said with one eyebrow pushed way up.

"No whacking," said Kristy laughing, "But I get it. Believe me." Kristy stood up from her chair. "You ready to ride?"

"I sure am." Megan stood and steadied herself. "Let's go."

AFTER TREVOR HAD WATCHED KRISTY GET INTO HER car at the Frontier, he'd gone home and landed on his couch, streaming every single movie made about Vietnam. Like he really needed anything more to make him feel like shit.

That was three days ago.

His thinking was already in the shits, when he commenced reliving every horrible detail relating to Carrie's sickness and death, available in his brain pan. Then, of course, that turned into a grizzly merry-go-round, that threatened never to stop. The same helplessness that had plagued him throughout Carrie's experience had returned, wrapping around him like a python.

With a huge sigh he turned and gazed out the front window. *I love Kristy.* Admittedly, he'd loved her ever since he beaned her with that loaf of bread.

He loved her and he was terrified. *Can I really go through all of that again?* How could he possibly watch another woman he loved suffer and die?

Incessant knocking at his front door pulled him out of his quagmire but thrust him into irritation. He was in no mood to deal with anyone. As he listened to the continued staccato cadence, he knew immediately who that was. Rob. Jesus that was the last thing he needed, another lambasting from that guy.

The incessant now-banging continued while he transferred onto his chair and rolled over to open the door. As he did, the stalwart form of his buddy came into view. He had his fists planted on his hips and a stern look on his face.

"Let me in, Trevor! You big asshole."

Whoa. All business. Taking a deep breath, he unlocked the storm door and rolled back a couple feet, motioning for Rob to come in. He rolled back over to the couch area and motioned further for Rob to sit down. "Would you like something to drink?" he asked trying to be hospitable.

Fists planted back on his hips. "I don't want to sit, and I don't want a drink."

"OK. What do you want?"

"What the f-fuck is wrong with you?"

Holy shit! First F-bomb the guy ever threw. "I don't know, I'm a mess, Rob."

"Yeah, a mess and a chicken."

"What?"

"You're a big scaredy cat, chicken!"

"You don't understand," he said looking down, subtly shaking his head.

"The hell I don't."

This guy was on a roll. "How do you mean?"

"I watched my Grandma Jane die. Slow and sad and bad. From a really bad sickness."

"I'm sorry, Rob."

"When I was little, she was the only one who thought I could do stuff. The only one who talked to me. L-like you and the guys talk to me."

"She sounds wonderful."

"She was *most* wonderful. It was so scary watching her feel bad, and then more bad. Getting skinny." Tears leaked out of his eyes, slipping down over his bright red cheeks. "I'm the one who found her. Not breathing, but her eyes were open," he said with his voice faltering, but still carrying on like a trooper. "You're being stupid."

"Yeah, I am."

"If I could have a person like her again, I would beg for that. Even though I know she would die too."

"You're braver than I am, man." With amazement and pride in his friend, he realized he'd never heard Rob say this much in one sitting before, and so emphatically.

"Bullshit! You are a war hero, Trevor. Kristy might have a war, too. She needs your hero stuff."

"Ok, Rob. You're right."

"Now, go take a shower. You stink," he said.

That made him laugh out loud. God, he loved this guy.

Rob stepped over and handed him a piece of paper. "This is the stuff about her test today. You better be there!"

Jesus Christ! This guy is a total badass. "Yes, sir," he said, saluting his friend. Rob saluted him back, then smiled for the first time since he'd gotten there.

"Hey wait, how did you get here?" The kid lived across town.

"I took the bus. Well... I took three buses."

"You want to stick around, while I get cleaned up? I can give you a ride home."

Rob hesitated.

"There is a new bag of hot cheese curls on the counter and a grape soda in the fridge."

Finally, Rob's stance relaxed, settled where he stood. "Ok," he said, as his shoulders dropped a little.

Trevor rolled over to him, reached up and rested his hand on the guy's shoulder. "Thank you, Rob."

CHAPTER 18

Lying on the clinic table, prepped and ready—*ready* was not at all what she was feeling about this next step in her life. Purposely distracting herself, she wondered what Trevor was up to.

She imagined him at the gym, at home, at the Nature Mart store where they first met. That last image made her chuckle. She'd never been hit in the head by a loaf of bread before. She missed him so, in spite of his asshole behavior. *I must be crazy.*

Before he disappeared like the jerk he was, she'd imagined him sitting in the waiting area with Vivian and Lucy. How could she have been so wrong about him? The same way she'd been wrong about Brad. She really did have crappy taste in men.

Those wonderful women out in the waiting room were her greatest supports. *Thank God for Lucy and Viv.*

FEELING EXACTLY LIKE THE DAY-LATE-AND-DOLLAR-short asshole he was, Trevor rolled into the waiting room of the day-surgery place, joining Viv and Lucy. They seemed truly surprised to see him. He was pretty sure they'd be there, because they were women of substance, and because of his cowardly retreat. Just the thought of that made him squirm in his chair. He should have been the one to stand with her, by her. Instead, he ran like a gutless asshole. Self-recrimination drenched him like a humid jungle storm.

Viv made eye contact, giving him a well-deserved glower, then dismissed him looking back down at her e-reader.

Lucy got up from her spot and came over, took his hand, giving his fingers a gentle squeeze. A soft smile of encouragement lit her face. "Come sit with us, Trevor. She went back a bit ago. I think this procedure takes about an hour."

"Sorry I'm late, there was an accident on the freeway."

Vivian looked up, smirking.

A little bit over an extremely awkward hour later, Kristy emerged from the recesses of the clinic. Her gaze down at the carpet, her face ashen.

He rolled forward a bit, the movement catching her attention. But, her expression showed even less than the puny bit of understanding he'd hoped for.

"What are you doing here, Trevor?"

Shit. "I've come to take you home and ...and be with you after this ...business."

She paused for what felt like forever, her expression unreadable. Well, she's thinking about it at least. Maybe? *Please say Ok.*

"Go home, Trevor, I've already got that covered."

Her words knocked the breath right out of him, like a full-on frontal take-down. He had to try hard not to gasp. *Oh, God. I'm so fucked.* As he watched the three of them gather up their stuff to leave, he struggled to breathe, seeing stars for Christ's sake.

Lucy, Vivian and Kristy headed toward the glass door exit.

Autumn sun shining through, blinding him. Lucy came over to him and leaned down, pressing her hand to his forearm. "Take it easy on yourself, Trev," she said, then straightened and rejoined the little group that he was less than welcome to.

After the door closed, he let loose the bonds on his emotions, and tears escaped. When was the last time he cried? When Carrie died. A giant sob shuddered through him.

The young woman at the front desk stood and leaned forward toward the glass partition. "Sir, are you Ok?"

He looked down at his hands lying clasped on his lap, tears hindering his vision. "Not at the moment, but I'll be fine." He used the heels of his palms to staunch the waterworks.

When he looked up the young woman had come around the desk, a couple tissues in her hand when she stepped up next to his chair. He looked up to her and took the tissues. "Thanks."

"Women sometimes have an intense reaction to the procedure," she said. She must have noticed his and Kristy's exchange after she came back out into the waiting area.

"Na, this one is all on me." He offered his hand for a shake. "Thank you, for your kindness. I don't deserve it," he said, taking in a full breath. "But I really appreciate it."

She smiled softly as she lifted her hand off his shoulder.

"I'll be OK." *Liar.*

———

KRISTY WAS UP EARLY, FEEDING THE GANG, TRYING to keep her thinking away from the possibly disastrous results of her biopsy. They'd said it would take three days for the results, and today was the day. Her anxiety had steadily mounted during the wait.

Houdini whinnied from the small training ring. She

looked out of the barn door to see him with his chest pressed up against the pipe fence, pawing at the dirt.

"I'm coming!" she hollered out his way. "Hold your horses!" She chuckled to herself.

Her cell phone buzzed against her right butt cheek, and she jumped. She pulled it from her pocket and dropped it on the barn floor, "Oh, shit." Retrieving it from the floor, she tapped answer. Her hand shook as she brought the phone to her ear.

"Hello, Kristy?"

"Hello, it's me," she answered, taking a big breath.

"It's Dr. Rodriquez. I'm so happy to let you know, everything is all clear. No bad cells."

Kristy let out a huge breath.

"How's the healing up going?"

"Not bad, really."

"Should be just about another week, and you'll be back to your old self."

When their conversation ended, she dropped to her rear onto a hay bale lying behind her. So relieved, she was light-headed. She had let her imagination go to lots of scary places that weren't at all helpful while waiting those three days. All those fears were whisked away, like clouds on a blustery New Mexico day.

She wondered what Trevor was up to. He'd looked devastated at the day surgery place. Served him right. He had no idea how devastated she was when he disappeared on her. *Jerk.*

CHAPTER 19

B ack at his condo, Trevor sat in his kitchen eating another tasteless dinner of eight ounces of chicken breast and a large tub of broccoli. He was so sick of broccoli he could scream. His nickel had been up with this prep shit weeks ago, and he still had a ways to go.

Then the mess with Kristy made things way, way worse than ever. How could things go from amazing to shit like that? Because he'd been an idiot-asshole, that's how. *Christ!*

It had been a week since he'd last seen Kristy at the place where she got her test. Her coming out of the back of that place, her exhausted, beautiful face—was so hard to see. Then when that most likely accidental, but tiny bit of happy-to-see-him look morphed into disdain and disappointment, it had been a huge punch in the gut. Still hurt like a mother.

He hoped like hell that she had gotten good news. Constant, low-level anxiety had plagued him ever since she'd shared with him about her questionable mammo. Constant worry about her and for her, over her maybe being terrified and dreading her future. He hated that he couldn't be with her right now, to help in whatever way he could. He'd do anything. But first he had to get her to talk to him.

He'd called and left so many unanswered voicemails, he was embarrassed at himself.

His world had brightened amazingly, with her in it. He desperately wanted all that back

Time for Plan B.

———

KRISTY HAD JUST RETRIEVED THE THURSDAY PAPER from her driveway and was about to turn and walk back to the house, when she noticed a white van with Happy Flowers Florist painted in orange and yellow on the side. When the van turned onto her driveway, she had a strong feeling that Trevor wasn't going to give up. She was still mad at him. Did he really think he could blow her off for a week, at one of her most difficult moments, and then show up to her test, and all would be hunky dory? *Bullshit!*

A young man with curly, black hair almost covering his eyes, jumped out of the van and jogged around to her with a big smile. He yanked open the sliding door of the van and leaned in. Retrieving a gorgeous giant bouquet of white tulips and hyacinths, with a bunch of baby's breath all around, he turned to her and presented the huge glass vase.

"Who are they from?" she said with skepticism, as she plucked the tiny envelope from its plastic stick.

The poor guy's face fell to the bottom of his chin. She bet he hated that part of the job, when recipients were underwhelmed.

She pulled the little card out of the envelope. *I'm so sorry, Trevor,* written there. For just a nanosecond, a pang of longing shuddered across her heart, but hurt let it shudder on by.

"Thank you," she looked at his nametag, "Gabe." She gave him her best encouraging smile.

She was still standing there, clutching to her the largest bouquet she'd ever received in her life when Gabe pulled away and disappeared back down her driveway. And dang, the thing was getting heavy.

No reason why she shouldn't enjoy some flowers brightening up her place. Although she was tempted, it would be a terrible waste to pitch them. She turned and walked back into her house, placing the arrangement on her coffee table.

Stepping over to the patio door at the back of her living room, she looked out over the pasture, where the horses were having a peaceful graze. Aggie had followed her into the house and sat down next to her. She lowered herself onto the couch and admired the flowers' addition of loveliness to her space. Then, noticing a little gold unicorn charm on a chain, hanging from one of the hyacinth stems, she leaned forward to get a better look. She'd always appreciated unicorns—horse plus magic.

Trevor must have noticed the several likenesses around her house. The framed diamond painting in the hall, the throw on her couch, the tiny statue on her bedside table.

Nope, the guy's a rat. She extricated the necklace from the flower, went into the kitchen, and stashed it in the little drawer of her desk nook.

LYING ON HIS BENCH INSIDE THE SMITH RACK, Trevor finished his last three-hundred-pound bench press. Rob sat on his stumps, to give him ballast. Facing the opposite direction, Rob chatted away on his phone with his new girlfriend, Amelia. He was quite the smooth talker from what

Trevor could glean from the conversation. *Good for you, Rob.* She'd been his prom date, and they'd hit it off.

Their happy deal delivered his thinking to his own miserable relationship situation. It had been three days, and he hadn't gotten any word from Kristy about her flowers. He'd even called the florist to make sure they had made it to her. Had insisted on talking to the kid who delivered them. Gabe had assured him she'd had the vase in her arms when he'd pulled out of her driveway.

God, he missed her. Things had just hit the sweet spot for them when he'd gone and fucked everything up by being an idiot coward.

How much time do any of us have, really? Christ, he wanted any time he could have with her, no matter how it was spent. He was done with any fear over her maybe being sick. No one had ever shared the results of her test. He guessed she'd made sure he was not on the receiving end of any of that information.

He had to get her back. He was a man on a mission, damn it.

"I'm done, Rob." The guy stood up, still talking to Amelia. He turned with a big bright smile on his face, pointing at his phone. Rob's joy pulled at his heart.

On to Plan C, he thought with renewed determination.

Chapter 20

Kristy pulled up to her driveway and jumped out to unlock the gate. A large boot-sized box leaned against the pipe fence. She couldn't remember ordering anything recently, but maybe this was some piece of clothing that had been on back order, that she'd forgotten about. *Who knows?* After opening her gate, she picked up the box and went around to get back in her truck. It was a little heavy to be clothing. *Hmm.*

She pulled up to the house and got out of the truck. Baxter chuffed from his spot. She went around and grabbed the box and her purse from the passenger seat and headed into the house.

With her interest and curiosity so piqued, she had to get into that damn box. She dropped her purse on the couch and went over to the kitchen table and placed the box there. Pulling scissors from the junk drawer, she proceeded to solve the mystery. When she lifted the lid, an amazing scent wafted up into her sinuses and all she could do at that moment was sigh.

Inside the box were six bags of fancy coffee. Her eyes

welled up when she realized one of the bags held her favorite flavor, piñon. One she had shared with *him* on one of those glorious mornings after an even more glorious evening.

After all the fun, the great sex, the meeting of minds, all the laughs and affirming quiet moments, why did Trevor have to turn out to be another man she couldn't count on? The universe really did play some mean tricks on you sometimes. Hot tears fell down her cheeks and onto her shirt.

After stupid Brad, wasn't she due for something real and true?

So much of Trevor, she had to admit, she truly loved. Really and truly. She grabbed a tissue from the box on the table where the house phone sat, wiped her eyes, and blew her nose. Her anger at Trevor had disappeared without her realizing. All that was left was sadness and an achy heart.

She took a deep breath, and letting it out slowly, she thought of Rob and that he would be there in a couple hours for a session—riding lesson really. The guy was getting so good and confident at handling a horse.

A new community support person had been hired for Rob last week, so she didn't need to worry about Trevor's blue-and-black van on her drive.

If she was honest with herself, she really would like to see that damn van coming up her driveway. Could she ever count on him again, though?

———

TREVOR AND MIKE SAT IN MIKE AND VIV'S DEN watching para-basketball on the tube, Mike drinking a beer, him tolerating another damn can of sparkling water. Sophie was down for a nap, so they had the TV down low.

He was *so* sick of all the prep crap. The glow of the whole bodybuilding competition deal had dimmed considerably. But he reminded himself, many of his fellow competitors were sick and tired of the whole idea by this point, too.

After the competition he'd be able to return to normal life. Well, as normal as possible with Kristy not being part of it.

"So, any news from Viv on how Kristy is doing? How the test went?"

"I told you the last three times you asked, I'm sworn to secrecy, bro."

"Damn," he muttered. "I'm going crazy with worry about her and that damn test. I want to be there for her, I don't care how bad it is, even if I have to go through the same thing or worse than I did with Carrie. I need to be with her, damn it!"

"I'm sorry. I promised my wife I wouldn't spill any beans and I'm going to stick with it. Vivian is still *really* ticked at you." He took another swig of beer. "And I have no intention of putting myself in that woman's line of fire." Mike grinned.

"Yeah, I get it," he looked down at his sparkling water, wishing it was a big shot of Jack. "I hate that she hasn't worked out with us since I played the coward card."

"Sorry, man." The look of pity on Mike's face was just plain humiliating.

He hated not being able to explain to Kristy how he was feeling, that he was sorrier than he'd ever been in his life about anything, that he'd played the giant asshole. But that wasn't who he really was. He needed the chance to prove that to her.

He didn't have a Plan D in his mind yet, but something would come. Hell, he'd go through the entire alphabet if he had to.

LATER THAT WEEK, TREVOR WAS ROLLING TO THE checkout counter at Home Fair, with his newly acquired navy-blue bathroom towels on his lap. He got to the end of the aisle and sitting there on its butt, looking just like Houdini, was a five-foot-high stuffed horse. It was gray with a white mane just like Houdini, too.

An absolutely ridiculous plan formed in his head, but he was desperate. Plan D!

He rolled over to the smiling stuffed Houdini look-alike and pulled up the price tag to get a look. *$350.* He'd pay twice that if she'd just hear him out.

He cruised to the closest clerk to state his intentions. They clipped the tag off for him to take to checkout and made arrangements for him to pull his van out front, where store personnel would meet him. He paid for everything with his card and headed out to his van, all the while thinking this was probably the stupidest idea he'd ever had. A total long shot. What if she didn't even like stuffed animals? Desperate times and all that, right?

As he engaged the lift, he tried to remember seeing any of them in her house. *Oh, yeah.* That tiny brown horse with grabby front legs, hanging from one of the lampshades in her living room.

No more worrying about that, or any other possible snags. He was a man on a mission. How he was going to get it on her property, he wasn't quite sure yet.

At this point, nothing would stop him.

CHAPTER 21

Kristy pulled up to her front gate. She noticed a disturbance in the dirt and dead leaves at the bottom of the fence to the right of the gate. Looking closer she saw a small slip of torn jeans fabric hanging from the top of the fencing. *Curious.*

With the gate finally open, she pulled through, her vehicle creeping toward her house. As she got closer, she noticed what looked like huge drag marks interrupting the smooth sandy dirt of her driveway. When she looked up from her driveway inspection, there on her front stoop sat a giant likeness of Houdini, with a big silly grin on its face. Baxter had taken up residence, his butt tucked up under it, lying between its front hooves. Aggie sat on the horse's left. They both gave her big doggie grins, hanging with their new friend.

Her heart pounded in her chest and her eyes welled up.

Somehow Trevor had gotten the thing out of his van, hoisted it up over her fence, then hoisted himself over the fence. Then dragged it, and himself, all the way to her front door. Then had to repeat the process, *sans* the horse, to get back to his van. *Unbelievable.*

She parked and walked closer to the spectacle, issuing a gasp, noticing a few drops of smeared blood on her stoop. Then she remembered the fabric on the fence. Making further inspection of the stuffed horse she noticed the left side of it had sand embedded in its fur from top to bottom. A crumpled note, on notebook paper, safety-pinned to the horse's chest, read, *I'm so, so, so sorry. Please give this old war horse a chance to explain.*

When she reached up to pet toy Houdini on the nose, happy-sad tears raced down her cheeks. Then she leaned in and hugged the damn thing around the neck.

TREVOR SAT, HIS STUMPS STRADDLING THE BENCH. He finished up his last set of overhead presses and placed the dumbbells on the bench in front of him. Raquel came over, placed both hands on his shoulders, and leaned in. He placed his hand over one of hers. She'd worked so hard to get to her current fitness level. Was a total trooper. He was sure she would do well at the show.

"It's not too long now!" she said right next to his ear. "Can't wait to get up on that stage." Her voice held such excitement.

He wished he felt more jazzed. He'd gone and banged himself up getting that horse onto Kristy's porch, tons of scratches on his arms, a nice two-inch-long cut on his thigh. Well, at least there was time enough for those things to heal up before the competition.

Every scratch was worth it. But he'd left the faux Houdini yesterday, and still no word. He was out of ideas, running out of hope.

He looked up to see Kristy marching toward them with great purpose. *Holy shit!* Her arms swinging with intent, hands in fists. She stopped right in front of them, crossing her arms over her chest.

"Move it or lose it, sister!" she said, addressing Raquel. The moment those words left her, her hand flew up to her mouth, as though she couldn't believe she'd said it. "Oh, God, I'm sorry about that."

Raquel issued an easy laugh. "No worries," she said, "Glad to see the big guy hanging out with someone with the same moxie." She raised her hand in a small wave, then returned to the rack she'd been using.

"I don't know where that came from," Kristy said, her eyes still wide.

"There is nothing going on with that young woman," he said, hands up in surrender.

"I know." Then she smiled and sat down next to him on the bench, resting her hand on his thigh.

He took her hand in his. "I never left you." He looked down at their joined hands. "I needed time to gird my loins." Looking up and into her eyes he swallowed hard. "So, what's the situation? Are we going into battle, together?"

"Battle, what? Oh, my God. You don't know?" She turned toward him, squeezing his hand with both of hers. "Mike didn't tell you?"

"Viv swore him to secrecy. I don't know anything," he said, squeezing back.

"There isn't going to be any battle, Trevor. I'm just fine."

His whole form, head to stumps, eased. He felt his shoulders drop from being up around his ears. "Oh, thank God. I was so worried about you. Jesus!"

"I'm not going anywhere." She pulled in a bolstering breath. "But I'd like to go everywhere, with you."

He palmed her cheeks and kissed her with everything he had.

Clapping, woo-hoos, and wolf whistles erupted all around them.

They parted from their kiss laughing.

Epilogue

That next April

All tricked out in a tux, Trevor stood under the ribboned tulip-and-hyacinth-laden arch. The minister stood facing the guests. Mike was right behind him as his best man, and in case he lost total balance to keep him from ending up on his ass.

He'd checked with VA Physical Therapy right after Kristy had asked him why he didn't use prosthetics. After pondering for a while, he'd thought, why not give it a try? Turns out these new legs were *way* easier to maneuver than the ones they tried to set him up with back in the '70s. Looks like you *can* teach an old war horse some new tricks.

Kristy had set up the barn for their wedding. When she first suggested it, he'd thought, no way was he getting married in a barn. But she'd convinced him and transformed the place into something just perfect for them.

The long wide, hallway between the row of four stalls and the north wall was perfectly set with chairs with gold covers. The arch was set up at the closed back door of the building.

Notes of the traditional wedding march sounded, and he looked to the back seating area for his soon-to-be wife. She stepped out of her little office where she'd gotten ready and was a vision in her cream-colored, satin coat dress. *Beautiful.*

The moment she saw him, confusion appeared on her face, then her eyes popped wide in realization.

He'd wanted the legs to be a surprise.

Kristy practically race-walked to get to him. Tears leaking from her eyes, as she stepped into her place facing him. He took her hands.

She pulled him down to whisper, "Wow, Trevor. You're tall." Her eyes huge.

"I wanted to stand with you, for this."

She wrapped her hand behind his neck and brought his mouth down to hers for a kiss.

"Hey, you can't do that until after the ceremony!" Vivian called out from behind her hand.

Soft laughter from the guests wafted around them.

Trevor smiled down at her and squeezing her hand he took a step toward the minister. "Here we go."

With Houdini whinnying from the training ring, Kristy smiled and stepped up, taking her place right next to him.

About the Author

Barb Simmons is an award-winning author of contemporary and paranormal romance. Growing up a Military Brat and having had the opportunity to live abroad and travel extensively has afforded her the chance to experience many exotic locales, the ultimate of which is one of the most romantic cities in the world, Heidelberg, Germany. Those experiences have influenced her work in a big way. Believe it or not, her prom and graduation were held in a castle.

Finally settled, she's put down roots in New Mexico's lovely Rio Grande Valley with her husband Charlie. They enjoy a quiet life in the country, with their two head strong canines, Mabel and Lily, making regular sojourns into the wonders of New Mexico and the Great Southwest.

www.ingramcontent.com/pod-product-compliance
Lightning Source LLC
Chambersburg PA
CBHW071720140626
46557CB00012B/985